YA

teenie

teenie

CHRISTOPHER GRANT

alfred a. knopf
new york

To Uwingablye Sowo

teenie

Chapter 1

"It's better to be a good listener than a good talker, because the good listener can remember what was said." As hard as it is for me to admit that my father says anything that makes sense, when I apply that little ditty to conversations with my best friend, Cherise, he hits the nail right on the head. Whenever we do something that doesn't pertain to her, like standing in front of the study abroad office, she gets really antsy. Most times it's a lot of eye-rolling and an occasional huff, but today she doesn't last more than ten seconds before she says, "So why are we standing here again? For that nerd thing you're trying to get into?"

I look at her sideways and grumble, "Yes, for YSSAP."

"What's 'sap'?"

Cherise has been my best friend since the third grade, and

over the past six and a half years, this type of conversation has played itself out time and time again. I guess that's what I get for doing ninety-five percent of the listening. "YSSAP, Young Scholars Study Abroad Program."

"Sounds like loads of fun," she sighs.

"Don't be a hater because you can't get in. You wish you could go to Spain for free."

"Whatever. Like I'd want to be in Spain with a bunch of shribs."

"I'm not a shrib"—her latest term for loser.

"If you say so . . . So how long do you plan on standing here?"

"I guess until someone comes out of the office."

Apparently that's all she needed to hear. She starts tapping on the door, waiting about three seconds before knocking harder. "There ain't nobody in there, Teenie. Let's go."

Teenie, that's what my girls call me. I'm five feet and one-quarter inch, one hundred and one pounds, with all my books in my book bag and a pair of waterlogged Timberlands on. "But they're supposed to put the acceptance list up."

"Do you see anyone coming to the door?" She says this as we've put about twenty feet between the office and ourselves.

I turn and look back, but don't see anyone. "No."

"That's what I thought. If you want to get anywhere in this world, you gotta BE AGGRESSIVE! BE, BE AGGRESSIVE!"

"What the hell was that?"

"It's one of the cheers that I have to do for tryouts, which is why I don't want to waste time standing in front of that door with you when I should be practicing."

2

"What time do the cheerleading tryouts start?"

"In twenty minutes."

"Oh. Sorry." I'm not really into the cheerleading thing, but Cherise definitely has the look: long hair, light skin, and a big butt, an apple bottom. She has all the makings of a video vixen.

"I don't know why you're so scared to try out for the squad."

"I'm not scared." *I am* scared, but she doesn't need to know that. "I told you like fifty times I'm going to get my braces off."

"You're getting your braces off today?"

Make that ninety-six percent of the listening.

Since I've been home, I've been standing in the mirror, staring at my teeth. It took the dentist an hour and a half to take my braces off, but part of me wants to go back to his office and tell him to put them right back on. My teeth are gigantic, looking like some supersized Chiclets. They don't taste like them, though, since I've been rubbing my tongue across them for the better part of an hour.

I hate being wound up like this. These are the times that I need Cherise the most, but as usual, when I'm desperate for help, she's never around. It's not every day that a girl gets her braces taken off, and after three years of being called everything from Tin Grin to Metal Mouth, the least she could do is be online when she's supposed to be. Cherise was supposed to log on to Instant Messenger forty-five minutes ago. Honestly, she should know better.

I'll be pissed if she's on the phone talking to one of those meatheads from the football team or has me blocked so I won't see if she's online. There are ways around that.

```
Appletini: crystal u there?
Bottle of Crys: yup, sup?
Appletini: nuthin' much. u c cherise
    online?
Bottle of Crys: Nope
Appletini: k thanx. ttyl
```

Guess she really isn't online, so I have to sit here and kill time. There are about twenty other windows flashing. I don't feel like chatting to any of my cousins in Barbados. I have one of those families with like thirty-something grandchildren.

My mother thinks lack of education and birth-control methods are the reasons my father's parents had so many kids. She may have a point, but I kind of agree with my dad's take on the situation. He says, "It ain't got a ting to do wit birff control. Dem people [his parents] was so cheap, dey ain' want to pay nobody to tend dee land. So dey *make* dee servants."

My paternal grandparents had fourteen children. My father was the first boy, after four girls. He has told many stories about shucking sugarcane and how he has the calluses on his hands to prove it. He embellishes, claiming he had to walk ten miles to and from school each day, uphill in both directions. I know he worked hard when he was growing up, busting his hump so we would have a better life than he did. Despite his family being well-off, nothing came easy for him. I think he works too hard, but that's all he knows.

Now I definitely don't feel like chatting to my cousins in Barbados. They'll want to know when I'm coming down and then ask me to bring them some clothes. They never give me any money to pay for stuff, always asking for designer T-shirts and things like that, like I'm some kind of millionaire. I'll kill time until Cherise gets online and chat with Garth. As annoying as he can be sometimes, he's the lesser of two evils versus my horde of cousins.

I told him I would be right back about an hour ago. He's written close to ten replies, giving updates on what he's doing. I don't even know why I gave him my screen name. Oh yeah, he helped me study for a math test, and I stink at math.

Honestly, I don't see the point in studying numbers. Isn't that why man invented calculators? I needed to pass an algebra exam to keep my ninety-three cumulative average and Garth gets hundreds all the time so you do the math. They call him Girth at school, and the name is well deserved.

My boy has a huge buffalo butt, looking like he's got two volleyballs tucked into his pants. People pick on him all the time at school. Someone stuck a WIDE TURN—DO NOT PASS ON THE RIGHT SIDE sticker on his lower back last semester. I had to try my best not to laugh before I pulled it off. I guess I can talk to him for a little while.

Scratch that, Cherise just logged on.

Appletini: Took u long enough,
     trollop. Where u been?
Cherish me: What?
Cherish me: What's a trollop?

Appletini: Look it up.
Cherish me: K hold on.

Five, four, three, two . . .

Cherish me: Oh u r wildin' out u . . .
  wait lemme get a synonym.
Cherish me: u harlot.
Cherish me: Who u think u r callin' me
  a Ho? ☹.
Appletini: lol
Appletini: Well how did it go?
Cherish me: I made the first cut.
Appletini: congrats!!! ☺☺☺
Cherish me: thanx. Still got one more
  to go though.
Appletini: Oh come on u know ur gonna
  make it.
Cherish me: probably, judging from the
  competition.
Cherish me: You should have tried out.
  I'm telling you. You woulda made it
  easy.
Appletini: Nah. I'm fine. That ain't
  my cup of tea.
Cherish me: u wouldn't believe how
  many dusty chicks were out there
  trying 2 get on the team.
Appletini: For real? Like who?

Cherish me: The head girls cut some of
  those dump trucks before they even
  started dancing.
Appletini: Like . . .
Cherish me: Keep your panties on geez.
Cherish me: I was writing the names
  but u so impatient.

Pause. Now see, this is the kind of stuff I hate. Instead of
writing all that crap about keeping my panties on, making me
wait, why not write the names of the girls down?

Appletini: u realize that all the time
  u wasted telling me 2 have patience u
  could have been writing the names of
  the girls.
Appletini: lol
Cherish me: lol. u r the worst
  sometimes.
Cherish me: Be playin' yourself too.
Appletini: how?
Cherish me: y u care so much who made
  the team if it aint your cup of tea?
Appletini: No reason. I just wanted to
  know is all.
Cherish me: Whatever.
Cherish me: OK back 2 the dump trucks
  that thought they had a chance in
  hell of making the team.

About time, geez.

Appletini: Who else was there?
Cherish me: Ugly Wanda and her friend
    with all the bumps on her face.
Cherish me: What's her name again?
Appletini: Who Lucresha?
Cherish me: Yuck. Well at least her
    name fits her busted grill.
Cherish me: u would think some people
    heard of Clean and Clear before.
Appletini: LOL!! ur wrong for that.
    lol
Cherish me: lol
Cherish me: Well it's the truth.
Appletini: Yeah I guess.
Cherish me: Speaking of grills . . .
    your braces?
Appletini: Finally got them off. Thank
    God.
Cherish me: Well make sure u scrub
    them teeth cuz I heard they leave
    spots.
Appletini: Shut up.
Cherish me: lol

I didn't have any spots, luckily. I brushed my teeth after
every single meal, even if I just ate a mint.

```
Appletini: My teeth look really big ☹
Cherish me: what u expect?
Cherish me: you got used to lookin at
    them with the braces on.
Appletini: I guess . . .
Cherish me: so you'd rather them be
    back on?
Appletini: Hell no!
```

Those things hurt like hell, all that adjusting and tweaking, and more adjusting, not to mention having to keep myself from eating certain foods. I wolfed down like three pieces of corn for dinner tonight.

```
Cherish me: Alright then. Stop
    complaining.
```

"Martine!!!"

"Yes, Daddy?"

"Get off dat computer and go and read a book!"

My dad needs to come up with some new sayings. He knows I've read just about every book in this house. "Okay, Daddy. I'm just finishing up my homework. I'll be off in ten minutes."

```
Cherish me: So what r u wearing
    tomorrow?
Cherish me: u there?
```

Cherish me: HELLOOOOOOOOOOOOO!!!!!
Appletini: Here, here, sorry.
  Beresford was complaining.

What the hell kind of name is Beresford? How could my grandmother do that to my father? Well, how could my grandfather's mother do that to my grandfather? My dad is a Third: Beresford Amadeus Lashley III, born and raised in Barbados, now the proudest Bajan in all of America. Barbados is nice and all, but I can't take them mosquitoes and I can't understand what my cousins are saying half the time. My family there uses curse words for the smallest things. Don't let them get angry, because they're liable to lob some serious vulgarity, the harshest being "God blind yah." That's deep.

Appletini: I'm not sure what I'm
  wearing.
Cherish me: Teenie, come on now.
Cherish me: u've been looking
  forward to getting those train
  tracks outta your mouth for so
  long now.
Cherish me: You better come to school
  looking right.
Cherish me: Why don't u wear your Wade
  jersey dress?
Cherish me: It's supposed to be nice
  tomorrow.
Appletini: 70-something degrees.

Beresford has a bunch of theories as to why it's so warm in the beginning of March. He's looking into buying land in the Midwest because he's convinced that it will be beachfront property in the not too distant future.

```
Cherish me: right so u can show a lil
   skin in that dress.
Appletini: u sure it aint 2 tight?
Cherish me: Duh, that's the point. No
   more using ur braces as an excuse to
   not take care of urself.
Cherish me: Put ur hair in cornrows.
   I'll do mine the same way and wear my
   Lebron jersey dress.
Appletini: u sure I'm not 2 skinny?
```

I've never worn that thing before. Honestly, I can't believe I even bought it.

```
Cherish me: ur small but u got a tight
   little body. I don't understand why u
   always wearing all them big clothes.
Cherish me: Watch tomorrow and see how
   the boys are sweating u.
Appletini: Okay.
```

"Martine!!! You ain't hear what I tell you? Come off dee friggin' computa now!!! You burnin' up all dee current! You ain't got to pay the bill, so you ain't care!"

```
Appletini: Hey, I gotta go. Beresford
   is barking.
```

The Bajan accent is coming out kind of strong now, a tell-tale sign that he's getting pissed off. The way he gets sometimes it's hard to tell he's been living in this country for over twenty years. I'm burning up all the current? Good Lord, give me a break. For some reason, he seems to think that we're going to run out of electricity soon. His new excuse for being such a cheapskate is that we're trying to go green. I'd better get off before he has a stroke.

```
Cherish me: lol. K. I gotta go anyway.
   Big Daddy just logged on.
Appletini: U still talking to that
   clown?
Cherish me: Don't hate, congratulate.
Appletini: lol whatever. ttyl c u
   tomorrow. luv u
Cherish me: luv u 2
```

Big Daddy is some college kid that Cherise met on Facebook. She's never seen him face to face, but he looks good, judging from the pictures on his profile page. He gets her whatever she wants, sends her jewelry, clothes, money. I tell her to be careful, because I think Big Daddy's gonna want something in return one day. Still, sometimes I get a little jealous. Why can't I have a Big Daddy in my life?

"Martine!!!!!!"

"Daddy, I already logged off, okay?"

It's a no-win situation with Beresford. He complained that I was running up his phone bill, so he made up a two-minute rule. The man would bust out a stopwatch and start a countdown when ten seconds were left. When I asked him for a cell phone, he looked at me like I had an eye on my forehead. Then I started using Instant Messenger. Now he complains about me being on the computer too much, saying, "You gine burn holes in yah retina starin' at dat idiot box."

He never seems to complain when I type up a work memo for him. Watching him try to type is so funny. He might as well use his feet. It's so pitiful that I almost feel like I have to help him. I type close to eighty words a minute, thanks to staring at the idiot box. I do get something out of helping him. He's a compliance officer with the Securities and Exchange Commission, so I get to learn some cool new words, like "capitulate." If I spend any more time trying to figure out my dad and his quirky ways, I'll end up in a mental institution. It's getting kind of late anyway. I better start braiding my hair. I wanna make sure I look hot tomorrow.

Chapter 2

As far back as I can remember, every morning my mother has woken me up by singing softly over my bed. Don't even ask me to try and sing the way she does. I think that stuff skips a generation or something. It's usually a Bob Marley song, most often "Three Little Birds." Glory Lashley's name should be up in lights, but three young children put an end to those dreams.

She's been a nurse at Maimonides Hospital since my twin brothers, Bakari and Solwazi, were born. Lucky for them they're twins, or we'd be talking about Beresford IV. My dad didn't think it would be fair if one had the "privilege" to be his namesake and the other didn't. That's why my name is Martine. It was his grandmother's name, and since he missed out with the boys, he made sure to leave some kind of mark on me.

It must've meant a lot to my father to be able to name me after his grandmother. She was a big part of his life. I'm not complaining, because Martine's not a bad name or anything. It's different, so I guess that's kind of cool, and it's better than the alternatives. If not for my older sister, God rest her soul, my name might have been Beresforda. My brothers warned me never to talk about her in front of Mommy and Daddy. The one time I did slip up and talk about her, Beresford started tearing up.

Kari and Wazi (those demons) are four years older than I am. They're freshmen at the University of Maryland, and I'm glad they're gone. I don't miss their loud mouths and smelly gym shoes. They also have a habit of farting without any sort of warning, the silent, violent joints that can clear a room full of people. I don't know what they eat, but whatever it is has to be rotten. My dad calls them toxic boxies, and he's right, because the stink that comes out of their butts has to be some kind of industrial waste.

After waking me with her sweet voice (Anita Baker ain't got nothing on my mom), my mother kisses my forehead and heads downstairs to fix Beresford his breakfast. She does this after working the graveyard shift, but just like my morning melodies, my father's tea and food are always waiting for him on the kitchen table, along with the morning paper.

My parents have this weird but romantic relationship. Because they work opposite schedules, him during the day and her at night, they only see each other for about thirty minutes in the morning and evening. When Beresford's waking up and she's coming in from work, they sit on the couch and talk about each other's day. When he's coming in and she's on her way to work, he'll get her a flower or some candy. The worst part is how they hug and kiss each other like they've been apart for years. It makes me want to puke.

I love my mother, but I couldn't be her. How she deals with my dad at all, let alone kisses him, is something I'll never understand. One week she was sick, and my father didn't know what to do with himself. Damn near burned down the house making tea. How the hell can you almost burn the house down boiling water? The firemen and police asked the same question. That black spot on the wall behind the stove won't go away, no matter how many coats of paint Beresford puts over it.

I try not to bring that incident up too much. I don't need to hear him start flipping out, calling me lazy and whatnot. He tried to say it was my fault because I wouldn't get up and make it for him. Okay, buddy, try again.

My father is old-school, always making comments about men and women having different roles and how women are supposed to carry themselves a certain way, some crap like that. That's why I have to make sure he's long gone this morning before I even think about putting on my Wade outfit. He would flip if he saw how tight it is. I'll have to rush home from school too, make sure he doesn't catch me hoochied out. I've never dressed like this, and I am not about to get caught.

I'll stay in the shower until he leaves. That won't seem unusual, because I take long showers at least twice a day, more in the summer. Of course Beresford complains that I've got the water meter spinning. He never stops complaining, ever.

My mother always tells me, "Cut your showers down a little bit and you won't have to hear him get upset."

She and I both know that even if I cut the showers down, Beresford would find something else to beef about. He'd probably say something about me not washing myself properly.

The long showers—I have to blame my brothers for that one. They traumatized me as a little girl. They would tell me that my shoes would smell just like theirs, that I would pass gas just like they do. I'm very particular about my hygiene. I just can't risk it.

I get out of the shower in time to hear Beresford belching like an ox and singing some old Calypso tune in the kitchen. With the example he sets, it's no wonder my brothers are two pigs.

"Da beach is mine!
I could bathe anytime!
Despite what he say!
I gon bathe anyway!"

I think that's the chorus of whatever song he's singing. That means he's finished with his tea and about to leave for work. Now I can start getting dressed. I have the outfit laid out on the bed. My braids are tight. I slept with a head wrap on, resting my face against my hand so one side wouldn't get messed up.

The texture of my hair is so weird, a mixture of about five, six different nationalities. I get West African (slaves in Barbados [Dad] and Grenada [Mom]) from both parents, Irish and Carib Indian from my dad, and Portuguese and Syrian from my mother. I'll be lucky if these braids last the day.

Whenever I look in the mirror, I can see little traces of my ancestors. My bronze complexion, like my hair, is probably from the mixture. My full lips show my West African heritage, and my straight, narrow nose has Western Europe all over it. When it comes to my green eyes, well, I haven't been able to pinpoint that one yet. I really don't like the way I look because I look so . . . different and mixed up.

My mother has always told us to be proud of our unique lineage and made a point to tell us about our ancestry. She says it's important, something about if you don't know where you come from, you won't know where you're going. Well, I know if I don't get going, I am gonna be late for school. It's time to put the dress on.

I look pretty damn good, if I must say so myself. The dress fits me well, a little snugger than when I first bought it, but I guess that's a good thing. I didn't think they made clothes small enough to be tight on me. My booty is definitely looking perky in this thing. I have on my silver hoop earrings, the ones with the studs, and a pair of white Pumas. I don't want to go overboard with the makeup, so just a little dab of lipstick. I call Cherise and tell her to meet me in the subway. I think I'm ready, maybe.

"Now see, Teenie!! I told you that dress was hot. Look at you."

Cherise has a huge smile on her face, even though her eyes are bloodshot red.

"Thanks." I'm blushing, trying not to look too nervous.

She blows her nose into the most saturated snot rag I've ever seen. I hand her a Claritin pill and take some tissues out of my book bag because the paper towel she's using is on the verge of disintegrating. Cherise and pollen spores don't get along at all.

"Thanks," Cherise says. She leans toward me and says, "In like five seconds, turn your head and look on the other side of the train."

"Okay." I wait, and when I turn, I see some boys standing on the other side of the train. There are a few of them staring at me, licking their lips and tilting their heads to the side, trying to look sexy.

"Don't stare too long 'cause they ain't that cute, but that's what it's gonna be like today. You watch."

A few years ago my mother sat both Cherise and me down and explained to us why we should stay away from the bad boys, the thugs that every other girl seems to lose their mind over. She told us that those boys were at their peak and that they had no room to grow. They won't have anything going for them once we get out of high school.

Her little speech worked on me, but Cherise loves her some thugs—only the pretty ones, though. As long as they come with the basics, starting with fresh shape-ups and crispy sneakers, they got a chance to get some vibes from my girl.

I don't know what kind of boys I like, but I know the kind I *don't* like. Unfortunately for me, those are exactly the types that always come up to me. Either they're supernerds like Garth who know the square root of every number from one to one thousand, or they have their pants hanging off their butts and their breath smells like goat cheese.

It's not like I want boys to talk to me anyway. I wouldn't have any idea of what to say because, well, I haven't had much practice. On the rare occasion that they do speak, it's to tell me to take my fake green contacts out. I guess I'm a little too homely for them to believe that my eyes are real. One kid said I reminded him of his mother, like I should be in the kitchen baking some cookies or something. He looked confused when I walked away from him. I guess he thought that was a compliment.

Today, it's a different story. I'm sharing the spotlight with Cherise. Usually, when guys come up to us, I am the one that they have to keep busy while they work on her. They talked to me because they had to. I didn't mind playing second fiddle, so I guess it's only natural that I feel uncomfortable with all the attention. Maybe I shouldn't have worn this dress.

"Ugh, my allergies are killing me," Cherise whines, blowing her nose. "My eyes feel like they're about to explode."

Cherise must be blowing a little too hard, because the lady next to her starts cowering away and covers her nose with her finger. Cherise is busy cleaning up and doesn't notice. A seat opens up across the aisle, and the woman jumps up from where she's sitting. She knocks a man's video player out of his hand, and he yells, "Damn, lady! Take it easy."

Cherise looks up just in time to catch the woman giving her a dirty look. "Why is that lady looking at me like that?"

"She was covering her face and looking at you like you had swine flu."

"For real? Whatever."

I keep my eyes on the woman, and sure enough, she looks

up at Cherise again, shaking her head with disgust. I don't know what her problem is, like Cherise having allergies means she's radioactive or something. I can't stand people like that. I wish there was some way I could get back at her.

I smile when I realize what she's reading. I turn to Cherise and whisper, "I read that book."

"Which one, the one that lady's reading?"

"Yup. It was good too, one of those thrillers where they keep you guessing right up until the end."

"Really? How did it end?"

"The main character's family dies in a plane crash, and he jumps off a bridge."

"Word?" Cherise gets a look on her face like she's plotting something. As we get up to leave the train, the woman flashes one last nasty glance in our direction; exactly what Cherise was waiting for. On our way out of the door, Cherise leans over to the woman, points at her book, and says, "He dies in the end."

It feels like ten thousand eyeballs are following my every move. Brooklyn Technical High School, Tech for short, is a *ginormous* structure, one city block wide, two deep, and eight floors high. Four minutes never seemed like enough time to get to class, but today I can't wait to get out of the hallway. The older boys lurk around every corner and flirt with me one after the other. I thought I would enjoy it more, but the way they look at me makes me feel like they can see right through what little I have on.

There are boys grabbing at my arm, *pssting* at me, trying to get my attention. I try to keep my head down and walk as fast as I can. Cherise is no help. She is relishing the attention, which today is even greater than normal because of her tight dress.

I can see the doorway of my class. There's one more group of boys coming down the hallway, the only thing standing between me and that door, my forty-one minutes of safety. I go to drop my eyes, hoping they won't notice me. My eyes never reach the ground. I stop, and stare. The sight of him, the glow, the way the light hits off his face, the boy in the middle with the sleeveless V-neck sweater. His name is Gregory Millons.

He's six foot four, senior captain of the basketball team, and hot to death. He's smiling at me. The dimple on his left cheek draws my attention for a second, but then I lock eyes with him again. My feet are stuck to the floor. I don't think I would be able to move even if someone pushed me. My mouth is hanging slack and my eyes are open wide, really wide. I can't take them off him, let alone blink.

"Yo, son, come on." The boy who was standing on his right is talking from somewhere behind me.

"Y'all go ahead. I'll catch up." Greg never stops looking at me.

He's walking over to me, leaning down to talk to me. I can smell his cologne. It's making me dizzy; it's Issey Miyake. I bought it for Beresford last Christmas, but he never wears it. He should, because it smells sooooo good. My knee buckles when Greg leans in, reaches for my hand, and says, "Hi, cutie, what's your name?"

If I open my mouth, I'll throw up.

"Her name is Martine."

Cherise comes over to save me from embarrassing myself. He's looking at her and now at me. He says, "I'm Greg. I haven't seen you before, Martine. What year are you in?"

"She's a freshman, like me. I'm Cherise."

Now I'm looking at them, following their conversation about me but not participating at all. God, he is beautiful, and he's smiling again, a different expression this time, amusement maybe? Does he see me staring at him? Can he hear my heart pounding? He looks at me funny and says to Cherise, "What's wrong with her, she don't talk or something?" because I've suddenly become mute.

I try to take a chance, save some face, but pay for it with a dry heave. Cherise helps me out again.

"She has laryngitis. She won't be able to talk for a week or so."

I would never have thought of that one. He lets her finish, then turns to me, studying me. I like how he looks at me. I feel sexy.

"Hmm. That's too bad. I was gonna ask her for her math, but since she can't talk, guess I'll have to settle for her MySpace."

"She doesn't have one."

"Facebook?" he asks. Cherise shakes her head to that one too.

My brothers cyberstalked me right off MySpace, so I never bothered setting up a Facebook account.

"Well, I guess her screen name will work," Greg says.

He's so smooth and quick. He knows I can't talk, so getting my phone number would be pointless. Don't know that I'd give him my number anyway. I'm not trying to give Beresford any reason to start with the yelling.

I fumble with the pen Cherise shoves into my hand. I write my email address and Instant Messenger screen name and pass it to her. She looks at me like I'm retarded before giving Greg the small piece of paper. He looks it over and puts it in his wallet, satisfied, I guess. His eyes are on me. The smallest, sexiest grin breaks at the corner of his mouth.

"Appletini, huh? I'll link with you later tonight, sweetheart."

Cherise lifts my arm and helps me wave as he walks away.

Cherise starts running in place, smiling like crazy. I'm still in shock, so she sort of guides me into my seat. We have a couple of classes together, and first-period American studies is one of them. I still can't believe that Greg talked to me. It doesn't seem real, but every time I look up at Cherise, she has a dorky smile on her face. Now I have the same dorky smile on my face because the reality of it all is finally hitting me. Gregory Millons talked to me; that's right, to *me*.

I don't even groan with the rest of the class when Mr. Speight springs a pop quiz on us. He's one of my favorite teachers, so it doesn't bother me that he tries to keep us on our toes. He swears he's a comedian, and is always cracking some lame joke. The class is American studies, but on our schedule cards it says "American Stud," to save space. The first day of class

Mr. Speight pointed out, "Hey, they wrote my name on the class schedule twice."

Corny, but from there, I knew he would be different. It's not hard to do well, since he keeps the material interesting.

This quiz is a joke, to be honest. Question 6 asks:

6. Which one of these names is *not* that of a Native American nation?
   a. Sioux
   b. Navajo
   c. Hellahwee
   d. Mohawk

Easy stuff, if you pay attention. I remember the funny story he had used that held the answer to this dumb question. He told us that it's politically incorrect to refer to Native Americans as Indians. First of all, the land of the so-called New World was nowhere near India. Second, he said, the people here were so distinct in culture and practices that it was unfair to lump them together with that incorrect name.

Mr. Speight mentioned the Blackfoot, the Sioux, and the Hellahwee as examples. Everyone in the class wondered out loud about the Hellahwee, having heard of the previous two nations. He said, "Yeah, the Hellahwee. The folks that get lost in the desert and say, 'Where the Hellahwee?'"

Everyone laughed. That's why I like him. He's not a prude like my other teachers.

I breeze through the quiz and look up to check on Cherise. She was one of the students who groaned the loudest when he sprung the quiz on us. Her pen just happens to be hovering over question 6 as she searches for the answer. Wow, I have to cough to keep Cherise from circling a. Oh my God, she needs me to cough again to keep her from circling b. She circles c. I stay quiet. Beresford always says she ain't wrapped too tight.

Chapter 3

Cherise and I meet up again fifth period for gym. Today is field hockey out in Fort Greene Park, so we both fake an injury. Her head hurts and my ankle is sore, or is it the other way around? The gym teacher (I can never remember his name) doesn't seem to care and leaves us on the sidelines.

Cherise has that dumb smile on her face again. "I know your head is all swoll up from Greg coming up to you today. Did you see what he had on?"

"Yeah, he looked nice in that sweater." Those chiseled arms have been on my mind all morning.

"The sweater was alright, but I was talking about his jeans."

"His jeans were nice." I really didn't notice them.

"Nice?! They were True Religion."

True who?

"Brand-new, limited-edition True Religions."

Nope. I still don't get it.

"They cost like three hundred dollars."

Oh! "Oh yeah. They were some hot jeans."

"Ice in his earrings and some hot Louis Vuitton shoes. He's fine, girl."

She stressed "fine," sounded more like "foyne." I was too busy looking at Greg's face to notice his jeans, but if Cherise says he was wearing three-hundred-dollar jeans, then he was. She knows more about fashion than anyone I know.

"He plays ball and he's a senior. Mmm. You're so lucky, Teenie."

Her eyes are staring up and to the left, at nothing in particular. I can tell she is in her fantasy world, probably doing some naughty stuff with Greg. Cherise is a bit more . . . advanced than I am, too damn fast, according to my pops.

"Why're you so quiet, Teenie?"

"No reason. Just chillin'." I haven't said much since this morning. I guess I'm still a little out of it.

"I know you're nervous and all, but you need to relax. Greg's probably gonna want to chat tonight. You can't be acting like no scaredy-cat."

The more I think about it, the more nervous I get. I know that tonight I will have to communicate with him. My "laryngitis" won't save me. "I . . . I don't even know what I'm gonna say to this guy."

"Just be yourself. Just write."

"About what?"

"Whatever comes to your mind."

"Why is he interested in me? Why does he want to chat with me?"

"Cuz you look good, dummy."

I swallow hard and say, "Cherise, I'm really scared."

She starts laughing at me and says, "Yo, what the hell is wrong with your face?" but starts patting my arm when she sees how upset I am. "Teenie, calm down. I got you. Don't I always have your back?"

I nod. Cherise always looks out for me.

"Well, here's what we gonna do. How about I sleep over tonight and I'll help you respond?"

I'm smiling like crazy. "That's a good idea. I'll call Beresford later and ask him if that's okay. Don't forget to ask your mother if you can stay."

Cherise waves off my comment. "Please. She don't pay no attention to me. She's all into her new boyfriend, Braxton."

I laugh at the way she says "Braxton." There's an uppity twang to her voice. Cherise forces a .smile, but I know she wishes her mother were around more.

The other girls are heading back inside. Cherise and I start to race back to the building and draw a curious glance from the gym teacher, Mr. What's-His-Face. I stop running and start limping. Taking my cue, Cherise holds her head and her belly, unsure of what BS she told him. Maybe I should be the one holding my belly, because I'm hungry as hell.

• • •

At Tech, the lunchroom is the place to be seen. Since I roll with Cherise, I get to sit in the cool section with other freshmen. We have to wait our turn before we can mingle with the upperclassmen. In our section, the middle of the northwest area, we sit with our clique: Crystal (aka Bottle of Crys), Sohmi, Malika and her twin, Tamara, and, last but never least, Sabrina.

Our area is prime real estate, not too far from the lunch line and within earshot of the football team. Today, for the first time ever, I heard them asking about me, the shorty in the Wade dress. Sabrina isn't too happy about that, since she always has to be the center of attention. She and Sohmi are practicing French for their class trip to Quebec on Friday. Malika and Tamara are going too. They've been pretty quiet today; probably that weird stuff where one twin is sick and the other one feels it.

Crystal smiles and says, "Damn, Teenie, you're looking hot today."

Cherise says I'm cuter than Crystal, but I don't see it. She has a lot of clothes and she really carries herself well. Her parents are supposedly rich, and she's an only child. She knows a lot of upperclassmen in school, so she is pretty popular. I heard something about her having an older cousin who goes to school here, but I've never seen her.

"Thanks, Crys."

"Yeah, Teenie." Sabrina's throwing in her two cents. "I didn't know you had any nice clothes."

Sabrina is, well, kind of a condescending cow. Even when

she's giving a compliment, she always has to slip in a slick comment. She walks around like she's better and smarter than everyone, like her butt cheeks smell like potpourri or something. She smirks once the spotlight is back on her and continues practicing her French.

"*Je m'appelle Sabrina. Je suis très jolie.*"

"What the hell does that mean?" Cherise scowls.

Sabrina smiles again, happy that she can do something Cherise can't. Malika picks her head up from the table and grunts, "She said, 'My name is Sabrina. I am very pretty.'"

Cherise rolls her eyes and says, "Oh my God."

I'm not even going to lie. Sabrina is beautiful, but conceited as hell. She's not as smart as she makes everyone think she is. Cherise saw her report card and said, "That thing had more seventies than a nursing home."

Sabrina and Sohmi are really tight, best friends like Cherise and me. When we first met, Sabrina called us Teenie and Meanie, making fun of what she called Cherise's "stinky attitude." She learned not to crack on us after that when Cherise called them Chopsticks and Sushi Roll. Sabrina is tall and skinny, and Sohmi is a short, plump Japanese girl. I'm busy trying to think of a snappy comeback like that when Cherise jumps to my defense.

"Damn, Sabrina. I don't understand you. Why you always gotta put people down? You stay trying to diss somebody, but then you forget to put lotion on your ankles. Looks like you been kicking bags of flour."

Everyone glances down just before Sabrina can shove her

feet under the table. Her ankles are ashy like an incense holder, so we all start laughing. I'm really laughing loud, because Sohmi says, "Hey, you got your braces off!"

I cover my mouth with embarrassment. My dress is no longer the subject of discussion, and everyone wants to see my teeth. Even Malika and Tamara manage to lift their heads off the table to take a look. Everyone is so impressed with how I look that Sohmi hasn't asked to copy my English homework. It's nice to not feel like a nerd for once.

"Teenie, can I get the English homework?"

"Sure." So much for that thought.

"I'm hungry." Cherise jumps up from the table and makes her way over to the lunch counter. I'm the only one that goes with her. When we get to the line, I glance over the cashier's shoulder and try to decide between the chicken and the fish. After I order the fish, Cherise leans in close and whispers, "I've been waiting all day to show you this."

She opens her hand and shows me a debit card. Her name, Cherise Taylor, is on it.

"Where did you get this?" I ask, checking out the card, looking for something that will show me it's fake. I don't even know why I ask, because I know whatever answer she gives is going to piss me off.

"Someone sent it for me, as a gift. There's five hundred dollars, and I can get whatever I want."

Alarm bells are going off in my head something awful right now. I scream, "What the hell are you thinking? You know this guy is gonna want something in return!!" By the starry look in her eyes, I can tell that she is thinking about giving it. That's right before she gives me that look that tells me to shut up and keep my voice down.

"Come on, Teenie, live a little. Seriously, what fun is life if you don't take risks sometimes?"

"What you mean? I take risks all the time." I pull my shoulders back and stick my chest out, trying my best to somehow look bolder.

"Yeah, right. The riskiest thing you probably do is go a day without flossing."

"Uhh, no. I floss once a day."

"Exactly."

"I was just joking." I actually floss twice a day.

"What're you worrying about anyway? He says I can get anything I want. That means you can get anything *you* want."

Hmm, this is true, this is true.

"I'm going to the mall after school," she says, which means I am expected to go with her.

"I don't wanna get in trouble."

"Don't be such a chicken. We don't have to pay for nothing, so what's the problem?"

"Maybe we should think this through a little."

"What's there to think about?"

"No one gives you five hundred bucks for nothing."

"Here we go," she says, rolling her eyes. "It's not that serious, Teenie. Just chill."

"I don't think this is a good idea."

"Well, I'm going. You do what you gotta do."

For half a second, I actually feel good about myself for standing my ground.

Then she says, "You know you have to follow up what you wore today with something nice. Can't disappoint Greg now, can we?"

"You know I hate you, right?" The way she said it too, with that tone that makes me want to choke her but always makes me tag along. "Let's not go crazy, okay?"

"There ain't nothing to worry about," she says, smiling at me.

She doesn't fight fair.

Chapter 4

"**W**hat is the largest inland sea on earth?" I know Garth will get the answer, but it was the only geography question I could come up with.

"The Caspian Sea," he yawns.

As usual, our biology teacher, Mr. Poretsky, is late to class. He's old, so we don't really give him a hard time. When he finally does walk into class, it takes him five minutes to get his papers out of his briefcase. He lets us talk until he opens his textbook and puts it on the desk. Once he does that, he's all business. Even though we start class ten minutes late, in terms of information flow, Mr. Poretsky's lectures are second to none.

When he's running extra late, like today, Garth and

I kill time by trying to stump each other with trivia questions.

"Your turn, Teenie. Let me guess. You're gonna pick literature, right?"

"Yup."

He clears his throat and says, "Ever has it been that love knows not its own depth until the hour of separation."

"Please. *The Prophet*, Kahlil Gibran."

"Man, this isn't fair." Garth is shaking his head. "I'm never going to get you with a literature question. I've been saving that one for weeks!"

"You can't pick a classic like that, silly. Your turn."

"The category is wildlife."

"What a surprise, but I got one for you."

"We'll see. Poretsky's almost done taking his papers out, so hurry up."

"Name three species of venomous mammals."

Garth's wide eyes give away his shock. He blinks a few times, trying to appear confident. "Wow, that's a good one. I'll get the easy one out of the way first. Platypus."

I wrote the answer down in my notebook. "That's one."

"Umm. Water shrew."

"That's two."

"And . . ."

I glance up at Mr. Poretsky. He's taking out his reading glasses. "You've got five seconds."

"Uhh. Uhh. I . . . I don't know."

"European mole. Gotcha!"

Mr. Poretsky places his textbook on the desk, and the whole class goes quiet.

Garth shakes his head and whispers, "Good game."

"Of course it was good. I won."

After bio is over, Garth walks me to the center section on the first floor. Cherise and I always meet there after school. I saw Garth looking at me in class today, more than usual. I think he likes how I look, but he'd never say anything to me. "Bye, Garth."

"Okay, Teenie. See you tomorrow." Garth will usually say goodbye and walk away, but today he lingers for a moment once he sees Cherise, as if deciding whether or not to speak to her. Her flared right nostril and slightly parted lips tell him to move on.

"Why do you even hang out with that big moose?" Cherise asks me, with Garth barely out of earshot.

"Shh!! He's nice once you get to know him." I turn around to see if he heard what she said.

"Hmm. Yeah . . . I guess I'll just have to take your word for that one."

"Shut up. Why you always gotta be so damn sarcastic?"

"Come on, Teenie, seriously, look at him. Look at his clothes. His pants are mad high. Okay, my man, where's the flood? Let's not even talk about his shoes. They're rocked over like he was mountain climbing or something. I wouldn't be caught dead talking to him."

I didn't even notice his pants today. I try to step in and defend him, but she's not quite done.

"And his butt. Look at his butt! He got more than me."

Cherise drops down and does a perfect impersonation of Beyoncé doing the booty bounce.

"Stop it, dummy," I say before I push her. I can't even lie. She has me dying laughing.

"Well, I guess I shouldn't be surprised," she sighs.

"Why's that?"

"You know what they say. *Nerds* of a feather flock together."

"For real? So why are you hanging out with me? Want some of that nerd to rub off on you?"

"Not quite," she snorts. "You're like my protégé, but based on the company you keep, it looks like I still got a lot of work to do."

"Yeah, whatever. So what're we doing now?"

"The mall, remember? I would've been done already if I didn't have to wait on your slow behind. I don't know why you had to be such a nerd and get a one-to-nine schedule." Cherise is shaking her head. I hurried down five flights of stairs as fast as my tight dress would allow. "Who the hell requests an extra class?"

"I told you already. I did it for YSSAP. Honestly, do you listen to a word that I say?" I've told her a bazillion times that I am trying to spend a semester overseas next year. I've been researching it since I first heard about it. The results were supposed to be up yesterday. Now I'm hearing that they will be up tomorrow during lunch, so I'll find out if all this hard work and sacrifice was worth it. That'd be soooo hot, if I could go to Spain. Taking a one-to-nine will feel a lot better when I get to practice my Spanish for real. Cherise cuts into my dream.

"Oh, change of plans. I can't stay by you tonight."

Talk about bursting my bubble. Now I have to talk to Greg all by myself. What am I gonna do now? "Why can't you come?" My arms are shaking, and she's smiling. Why is she smiling? Can't she see that I'm about to lose it?

"I'm going out tonight."

"Going out? On a school night? With who?"

As soon as she says, "Don't worry about it," I know that means she's gonna meet up with Big Daddy.

"I need you to cover for me, Teenie. I'm gonna tell my mother that I'm gonna be by you studying. Did you talk to your dad about me staying over there tonight?"

I almost want to say that I had told Beresford, to keep her from going to meet Big Daddy. I shake my head. "I didn't tell him yet."

She lets out a sigh of relief and says, "Good, because I don't want him asking no questions. Let's hurry up and get to the store."

This whole situation—the debit card, meeting up with *her friend*, the possibility of having to lie to cover for her—I don't like it one bit. There are too many things that can go wrong.

We decide to take the long way to the mall and stop at Golden Krust for some beef patties. The patty shop around the corner from my house is so much better, but for a franchise, Golden Krust isn't half bad. As we walk up Flatbush Avenue, it seems as if we get stopped every two seconds by some guy trying to get our phone numbers. I don't want Beresford embarrassing me, so I take theirs, even though I have no intention of calling any of them. No Greg Millons out here, although one guy did have some really nice teeth.

Cherise causes a mini traffic jam leaning into the passenger side window of some Jamaican guy's BMW. Not sure what gave away the fact that he was Jamaican—probably the green and yellow stripes on the side of his black car or his friend trying extra hard to get me to notice his accent.

"Yo, baby luv, you want a ride?"

Never mind that he's sitting in the backseat asking if I want a ride. I'm not going over there. Cherise doesn't seem to have a problem. She is leaning so far into the damn car that she might as well get in. On second thought, she better not get too close to those guys with the way her breath is humming. The stick of gum she has in her mouth is probably getting its butt kicked by spicy beef. She tore that patty up like a ravenous vulture. She's lucky I grabbed those extra napkins.

I sigh with relief when Cherise walks away from the car. She has a funny look on her face, so I ask, "What's wrong?"

"I was starting to catch contact." She's fanning her face.

"They were smoking weed in the car?"

"Smoking? Smelled like they were growing the stuff in there."

I laugh. "That's what you get for leaning up in his car like a prostitute."

Cherise pushes me and says, "Shut up." She smiles. "Yeah, I need to cut that out. As soon as I see a nice car, my eyes light up. I gotta be careful with that stuff."

Thank God she realized that on her own. I wish she would be as concerned about the other things that she's planning to do today. Before I get a chance to wrap my mind around that, Cherise starts bumping me, telling me to turn around.

"Look at *this* chick."

When I turn around, I see this chunky light-skinned girl waiting at the corner, crammed into a top and matching skirt that are at least three sizes off. She's wearing a small, while her exposed gut is calling for an extra-large. I know I shouldn't talk with my short dress, but there are some people out here that really don't know how to act at the first sign of warm weather. It's the beginning of March, and you would think it's the middle of summer with some of the stuff they're wearing.

Cherise is about to say something to the girl. I grab my best friend's arm before her smart mouth gets us into trouble. The girl's belly isn't the only thing that's extra-large. I think she would stomp the DNA out of Cherise and me. She doesn't notice us and gets into a dollar van that pulls up in front of her. It's kind of stupid to call a cab that costs two bucks to ride a dollar van, but that's been their name since I've been riding them.

I bet the driver couldn't wait to cruise around with the windows open blasting the newest dancehall music. Who needs an iPod? All I have to do is stand on the corner of a busy intersection and I'm bound to hear everything from R&B to reggaeton.

Honestly, when I see this, even the fat girl, it makes me love living here. This is just a typical day and there's so much life. I smile and take a deep breath and think, What's not to love about Brooklyn? A truck blows past, leaving me hacking in a trail of black smoke. I guess that answers my question.

41

Chapter 5

"Teenie! What are you doing? Will you come over here and help me?"

We're in a department store with all the name-brand stuff at really cheap prices. I'm supposed to be helping Cherise find clothes, but I've been too busy counting all the surveillance cameras. I may be no good at uncovering the top-quality clothing (because it's mixed in with the kind of stuff Garth would wear), but I sure can spot a camera. There are like twenty of them in here!

Cherise is a pro. While she dives right into the racks, I stand stiff and look around nervously, like I'm about to steal something. I can't put my finger on it, but something is just not right. I catch a few wary eyes from some of the security personnel wondering if I am up to no good. That's what this feels like: stealing. My apprehension only lasts until Cherise shoves a cute burgundy skirt into my hands.

"Oh, you're gonna try that on," she says with a smile before jumping back into the rack.

The next thing I know, I'm holding like seven outfits in my arms at the checkout line. Cherise has one or two more shirts than I do, and when we get rung up at the register, it comes to $484.61. Cherise hands the cashier the card. I'm just waiting for the SWAT team to come busting out of the ceiling. I hold my breath as the cashier swipes the card. Something's gonna go wrong, I can feel it. Cherise can see how nervous I look and elbows me in the side, giving me her *You better cut it out* face. The receipt starts printing, and I take a deep breath. We're home free.

Cherise gets hungry again, so I treat her to pizza at the café on Hanson Place. It's the least I can do after she hooked me up with the clothes. I can hardly eat, because my mind is on everything else but food.

"What is your problem, Teenie?"

I understand Cherise more from the look in her eyes than the words coming from her mouth. It's full of pepperoni and cheese. "Nothing, I'm just not that hungry."

She knows I'm lying, glaring at me while she drops her slice and wipes her mouth with one of the fifty napkins we've wastefully pulled from the dispenser. She sips at her Sprite, about three or four gulps, but her eyes stay fixed on me. She sucks at a space between her teeth before taking her finger to pry out the piece of tomato stuck there.

"You really gotta loosen up, girl. You act like such a shrib sometimes. I can tell what you're worrying about, so just stop it."

"What are you talking about? I'm fine." I'm trying my best to look comfortable. I even take a big bite of the pizza, but it's such a chore to chew it.

"You got some new clothes for free. Ain't nothing gonna happen when I go out tonight, and chatting with Greg is gonna be way easier than you think. Okay? Damn!!!"

That's why she's my best friend. She knows me so well, and as soon as she says that, the pizza's not so gross-looking anymore. I smile, showing some teeth, and she sighs loudly. I relax a little, and we lose track of time. We start going through each other's bags, making suggestions about how we should dress for school tomorrow. I have to admit we really got some nice stuff. "So what would I wear this with?" I'm holding up a tight brown T-shirt with a crazy-looking Afro chick on the front of it.

"Lemme see what you got in there." Cherise rummages through the bag and pulls out a tan-colored, half-cut Sean John jacket. "You could wear it with this."

"What about if I wore it under one of the button-down shirts I have at home but leave the buttons open?"

Cherise smiles and says, "Yeah, that'll work too. You can mix some of your geek clothes with what you bought, and it might actually look nice."

"True."

"I can't wait to see Sabrina's face when she sees your new style."

"I don't get that girl sometimes. Why is she so stink?"

"She's jealous of you."

"Of me?"

"Yeah, you're smart. She's dumber than dumb. I know I say some stupid stuff sometimes, but . . . What?"

She stops when my eyebrows shoot up. Talk about the pot calling the kettle black. "No, nothing," I say. "You were talking about Sabrina being dumb."

"Right. The next time she gets on you, you need to put her in her place."

"What, like say some jokes about her mother?"

"Nah, her mother's like some big-time model or something. Just stick with cracking on Sabrina. Say something like, 'Sabrina, you're so dumb, you spent ten minutes staring at a carton of orange juice because it said concentrate.'"

I shoot Sprite through my nose. That is hee-larry-us. "How do you come up with these things?" I ask, trying to dry the soda from my nose. It's burning!

"Come on, it's not that hard. Try it out."

"I can't think of anything."

"Just try."

"Okay." There is one that I made up a long time ago, but I'm not sure it's funny. "Sabrina is so dumb . . ." I suck my teeth and shake my head. "No, it's stupid, Cherise."

"Just say it."

"Alright, alright. Sabrina is so dumb that she had to do a project on euthanasia and she started talking about teenagers in Japan." The look on Cherise's face leaves no doubt that my joke missed the mark, even before she says, "I don't get it."

I try to explain it to her. "So euthanasia is assisted suicide, like mercy killing, and it sounds like 'youth in Asia.' You know, like kids in Japan or something."

She eyes me for a moment, then cracks a smile and says, "Hey, that's not bad" and giggles a little. "But I got a better one. Sabrina is so dumb she couldn't pour water out of a boot with instructions on the heel."

"Stop, stop," I say in between laughs. "I'm gonna pee my pants." She starts talking about Sabrina's ashy feet again and keeps me cracking up.

"They looked like they were ready to throw in the frying pan. Looking like she had flour and bread crumbs on her crusty feet."

"Have you ever thought about doing stand-up?"

"Maybe someday."

"Oh, my stomach." Cherise starts digging through her bag again, so I say, "Trying to figure out what you're gonna wear to school tomorrow?"

"Nah. I'll do that when I get home. I'm trying to pick out what I'm wearing tonight." My smile disappears. She pulls something out of the bag and asks, "How about this one?"

"That's nice." I'm not even looking.

"Ohh. This is even better. I forgot I bought it." I look up and see her admiring a black dress that fit her like a glove when she tried it on in the fitting room. I try to smile, even though that's probably the last thing in her bag I'd want her to wear. "I'm so glad you didn't tell your father that I was staying there tonight."

"Yeah, that would've messed you up big-time. OH, CRAP!!!!! Cherise, what time is it?"

"Five o'clock."

"Oh my God, I gotta get home." I totally forgot that I had to beat Beresford to the house. If he catches me in this dress, I am so gonna be dead.

Cherise and I hug and part ways at the train station. I'm in such a rush that I miss her cheek and kiss her ear. Cherise yells to me, "I'm gonna be online for a little while before I go out" while I'm running toward the turnstiles.

I turn and yell, "Okay" and knock over a little Asian man who sells DVDs on the train. He mumbles something, gives me a nasty look, and unleashes a barrage of words I don't know or understand. Cherise runs over and squats down beside him, yanking me down in the process. "Help him."

"But I gotta go."

"Now! Help him." She points behind me with her mouth, and I see Beresford going through the turnstile.

"Oh God, Cherise. What the hell am I gonna do?"

"Gimme your ID card."

"What?"

"Will you gimme the damn card?!"

Cherise and I trail Beresford, darting in and out of the shadows like a pair of hungry wolves. We're stationed behind a delivery truck while we go over the plan.

"Aight, Teenie, when that light changes, you get moving like a runaway slave."

The plan is for Cherise to jog up to my dad and tell him that I dropped my ID card. She's gonna stall him long enough for me to run around the block and beat him to the house. "Why can't you take my bags for me, Cherise?"

"I'm not taking those home. I don't even know where I'm gonna hide the stuff that I already have."

"I thought your mother didn't care about you getting new stuff."

"She ain't gonna be mad about me getting new stuff, she'll just take it and wear it herself. If those bags come home with me, you can kiss them goodbye."

I clutch the bags close to my chest.

"Enough talking, Teenie. If we don't time this right, you're dead. You ready?"

I take a deep breath and nod my head. The light changes, and Cherise starts jogging after my dad. I take off around the corner as she starts calling, "Mr. Lashley. Mr. Lashley."

I'm glad I wore these sneakers, because I'm moving like a cheetah. The only problem is I have to stop every now and then to pull my dress down. There are some nasty old men saying things to me. They're disgusting, some of them old enough to be my grandfather. I don't have time to worry about that crap. The only thing on my mind is getting inside that front door before Beresford spots me.

Since I'm stuck running with these bags, I wish I would've bought one thing that I could hide under, but everything is as tight if not tighter than my dress. Hopefully none of my neighbors are looking out of their windows.

My lungs are burning by the time I reach the front door.

I'm so used to putting my keys in my pocket that I'm patting my sides, forgetting they're in my book bag. It's taking me too long to get the book bag off because the shopping bags are around my arms. I'm looking down the block, hoping Beresford doesn't turn the corner. Okay, I have the keys in my hand. I'm almost inside, disaster averted. Out of the corner of my eye, I see the front door to my house opening. My heart stops, because my mother is standing in the doorway.

Chapter 6

People outside my family think my father's the one who runs things. Yeah, he yells a lot and gave out the spankings when I was younger, but it's my mother that's in charge. I can deal with my father's complaining. I'm immune to it now. Well, that's stretching it a little. Anyway, my mother has this way of looking at me that just makes me feel so small. We're the same height, but I feel myself shrinking with each passing second. I don't even have to meet her eyes to feel that gaze, that *I'm so disappointed in you right now* look. It seems like an hour before she finally speaks.

"Martine."

Ugh, the way she just said my name, no anger in her voice at all. It's that calmness that convinces me I'm in for it.

"Is that how you went to school this morning?"

I know not to say a word. I just nod my head, keep my eyes on the floor. Anything I say can and will be used against me.

"Hmph," she grunts.

I know she's smiling, but that's not a good thing. When my mother smiles like that, she is pissed. I'm breathing really heavily and I haven't even looked up at her yet. She's waiting for me to lift my head so she can finish scolding me. She won't move until I do. I look up, slowly, look away, and then meet her eyes.

"Don't *ever* let me see you outside dressed like that again. Do you understand me?"

My eyes are back on the ground. That "ever" had some serious emphasis on it. I might as well burn this dress, because I'm never wearing it again.

"Look at me when I'm speaking to you, young lady."

I look up. I'm close to tears. I hate disappointing my mother, hate having her upset with me.

"Do you understand me?" she repeats herself. That's never good.

"Yes, Mommy."

"Go inside and change your clothes."

"Yes, Mommy."

As I try to hurry past her, I bump her with one of the shopping bags. She is so upset by my dress that she hadn't noticed them until that instant. She puts her arm out, blocking my way.

"What's that?" she asks, pointing at the bags.

"Cherise and I went shopping today."

"Let me see."

I don't even put up a fight. I'm in trouble regardless, so it's best to just hand over the goods. She sifts through the bags, carefully checking the price tags on each piece of clothing.

"Martine."

Oh no. That voice again.

"These clothes amount to over two hundred dollars. Where did you get the money for them?"

"Cherise got them for me," I whisper, hoping she won't ask me again.

"Excuse me? I didn't catch that."

"I said Cherise got them for me." I make sure to keep any hint of annoyance out of my voice.

"Oh really?" Her eyebrows arch when she hears that. I look away and see my father coming up the block. I start crying and drop my head in shame. Now I'm really gonna get it, double-teamed. My mother sees him too. She shoves me inside the door and says, "Go inside and take that dress off right now. Take these bags and put them inside your closet, and don't touch them until I come home."

I'm nodding my head like crazy.

"We'll finish this discussion later."

"Yes, Mommy."

I fly upstairs into my room. Even though she's upset with me, she still covered for me. I love my mother.

My mother is still mad, because she didn't even give me a chance to apologize. She came into my room and handed me my ID card without saying a word. I sure am happy she didn't say anything to Beresford before she left for work. He would've lost it if he'd seen that dress. He did say something to my mother about "the slackness" that Cherise was wearing. I haven't heard much since then. He's probably on the couch snoring, with his feet jammed under the throw pillows. I swear the soles of his feet look like raw chickens.

Thank God Cherise just logged on, because thinking about Beresford's feet is starting to make me gag.

```
Cherish me: u get in the house ok?
Cherish me: I tried to stall him as
    long as I could
Appletini: yeah. thanx.
Cherish me: did he say anything to you
    about my dress?
Appletini: no
Cherish me: ok cool
Cherish me: what's with the one word
    answers?
Cherish me: u ok
Appletini: I'm ok. my head is just
    hurting me a lil bit.
Appletini: I think I pulled my braids
    too tight
Appletini: actually . . . I kind
    of want to talk to you about some
    stuff.
Cherish me: please don't tell me ur
    still nervous about talking 2 Greg.
```

Now why she had to go there? I wanted to talk to her about the new clothes and her leaving her house to meet with

Big Daddy tonight. I wasn't even thinking about Greg until she brought it up. And guess who just added me to their Buddy List?

> Appletini: he just added me 2 his
>   buddy list!!!!
> Appletini: gulp ☹
> Cherish me: you'll be fine. Just tell
>   me what he says when you get stumped
> Appletini: ok
> Multi-Mil: hey Ma what's da deal?
> Appletini: hey gregory. What's up?
> Appletini: I like your screen name.

I hope I didn't type back that response too fast, like I was anxious or something. He sure is taking long to answer. He must be slow on the keys.

> Multi-Mil: nuthin' just chillin'.
>   what's good wit you?
> Appletini: I'm fine.
> Multi-Mil: u like my name?
> Appletini: yup. It's cute and it
>   fits you.
> Multi-Mil: aight, aight. That's what
>   I'm talking about. So whassup wit u?

Okay . . . this is pretty easy. He's asked me the same question three different ways.

```
Appletini: nothing much just
   relaxing.
Multi-Mil: so how is your throat?
Appletini: my throat?
Multi-Mil: yeah, your larringidis.
```

Larringidis . . . wow! He's a senior and that's how he spells laryngitis? Ohhh-kay.

```
Appletini: it's feeling a lot better
   thanx.
Cherish me: Teenie
Cherish me: what's going on??!?!?!
   What's he saying?
Appletini: nothing.
Appletini: he's kinda dumb. He spelled
   laryngitis with a D.
Cherish me: AND?!?!?!
Cherish me: Teenie. Don't make me come
   over there and smack the taste outta
   your mouth.
Cherish me: I don't care if he spelled
   it with a y.
```

Hmm . . . didn't I just spell the word for her? I just spelled it!

```
Cherish me: He's the best-looking guy
   in school.
```

```
Cherish me: what r y'all talking bout
    anyway?
Appletini: He's asked me what's up
    like 3 times. What am I supposed 2
    say now?
Cherish me: Ask him how his day was.
Appletini: so greg how was your day?
Multi-Mil: It was cool. How bout u?
Appletini: It was ok. Same old
    same old.
```

BORRRRRING!!! I could have more fun watching paint dry. I'd rather watch my dad clean underneath his toenails.

```
Multi-Mil: So what would it take for u
    to have a good day?
```

Now that's more like it. I felt a couple of butterflies after that one.

```
Appletini: Cherise. He just asked me
    what would it take for me to have a
    good day.
Cherish me: Say, why u have something
    in mind?
Appletini: no come on. That's a little
    forward don't u think?
Cherish me: stop acting like ur
    5 years old.
```

I toggle back over to Greg's window and type in the response that Cherise suggested. I haven't pushed enter yet; I admit I am a little scared. Here goes.

```
Appletini: why, did u have something
    in mind?
```

I think I caught him off guard with that one because he is taking even longer to respond. Now I wish I hadn't written that at all, but I can't stop smiling, waiting to see his reaction.

```
Multi-Mil: I could think of a few
    things, but I ain't trying to get
    slapped. Lol
```

I pause here and think about how to reply. I don't want to come across as easy, but this is Greg Millons we're talking about. If he only knew how often his name came up at the lunch table. His perfect teeth, light brown eyes, body like an Adonis. Let's not even talk about how good he smells, MMM!!! He's chatting with me, flirting with *me*.

I know at least a hundred other girls who would kill to be in the situation that I'm in right now. I can't let this opportunity slip by. I know I'm lucky to even be talking to him. There's no reason to be scared. Being behind the computer is giving me more confidence anyway. I know I would be tripping over my own words if he were talking to me in person, but I'll cross that bridge when I get to it. I guess it's time for me to flirt back. It's now or never.

Appletini: I really don't think
    there's anything u could say that
    would get u slapped. ☺

Ugh, that came out sounding kind of dumb.

Multi-Mil: oh aight. It's like that?
    no doubt.
Cherish me: Teenie
Cherish me: hello . . .
Cherish me: Teenie what's going on?
Cherish me: HELLO HELLO HELLO HELLO
    HELLO HELLO HELLO HELLO HELLO HELLO
    HELLO HELLO HELLO HELLO HELLO HELLO
    HELLO HELLO HELLO HELLO HELLO HELLO
    HELLO HELLO HELLO HELLO HELLO
    HELLO!!!!!!!!!!!!!!
Appletini: sorry sorry.
Appletini: he's starting to get a lil
    risque.
Appletini: saying that my body is
    tight and that I got it going on.
Cherish me: see. now how long I
    been telling u 2 take care of urself?
Cherish me: u need to stop acting
    like a tomboy and start acting like
    a lady.
Appletini: hold up he's typing
    something.

I toggle back to Greg's box with eager anticipation.

Multi-Mil: yeah so when u walked past
    I was like damn, Shorty got a bangin'
    body.

That's the third time he's said that. Each time it made me feel better than the last.

Multi-Mil: I was wondering how come
    I never seen u before.
Appletini: so do u have a girlfriend?

I waited long enough to unleash that.

Multi-Mil: nah.
Appletini: Cherise, I just asked him
    if he has a girlfriend. He said no.
    Does he have 1?
Cherish me: I'm not sure. I ain't
    never c him with nobody but u never
    can tell.
Cherish me: Anyway I'm out.
Cherish me: Remember my mother thinks
    I'm gonna be studying by u so
    don't call here looking 4 me like an
    idiot.
Appletini: I thought she wasn't gonna
    b home

```
Cherish me: she and Braxton had a fight
   so she's up in her room all mopey.
Appletini: ur still going?
Cherish me: yeah
Appletini: how u gonna get back in?
Cherish me: I left the backdoor open ☺
Appletini: wait a second
Appletini: are you sure about this
Appletini: y r u going out so late
   anyway?
```

She logs off without answering. She's got to be crazy to go out this late. I'm too afraid to put the recycling out at night, let alone get on the train.

```
Multi-Mil: so what nationality r u?
Bottle of Crys: whaddup Teenie
Appletini: take a wild guess Greg
```

Crap! I hate when that happens. Crystal's window just popped up on my screen and I sent that to her by accident.

```
Bottle of Crys: what?
Appletini: oh sorry Crys. Wrong box.
```

I close out the window but it pops open right away.

```
Bottle of Crys: yo Teenie, who u
   talking about?
```

I close it again but Crystal sends me another message.

> Bottle of Crys: r u talking about Greg
>   Millons?

It looks like someone wants to get blocked. I shut Crystal down and turn my attention back to Greg.

> Appletini: I'm West Indian
> Appletini: half Grenadian, half Bajan
>   (Barbados)
> Multi-Mil: nice. an island gyal huh?
> Appletini: lol. yup
> Appletini: how bout you?
> Multi-Mil: my folks were both born in
>   NY but my family is from North
>   Carolina
> Appletini: ok
> Multi-Mil: u know u look good
>   right?
> Appletini: thank u.

I'm gonna go with it.

> Appletini: u got it going on urself.
> Multi-Mil: u think I look good?
> Appletini: yeah ur fine.
> Multi-Mil: u sure u only a freshman?
> Appletini: yeah. y?

```
Multi-Mil: cuz their ain't that many
   freshman shorties that be catching
   my eye.
```

Okay, I'll let that one slide. Lots of people confuse "their" with "there."

```
Appletini: ☺ thanx for the compliment.
Multi-Mil: and speaking of eyes . . .
Appletini: yes they're real
Multi-Mil: lol. guess you get that one
   alot.
Appletini: a lot lol
```

Had to correct that one, even if he doesn't know I'm correcting. "Alot" is one of my pet peeves.

I'm not even scared anymore. This is fun. Greg might not be the sharpest knife in the drawer but he is definitely keeping me on my toes with his comments. I'm pretty sure he does this kind of thing all the time, but whatever—he's doing it with me now, and that's all that matters. I want to make sure that my answers are on point, but I also don't want to sound like I'm trying too hard.

I glance up at the clock when I hear my dad shuffling up the stairs. Wow! I didn't realize that it was almost midnight. If Beresford sees me on the computer, he will cut the power cord. There's no way I can get into my bedroom without him seeing me, so I push the power button on the monitor, put my head on the keyboard, and pretend to be asleep.

"Martine."

"Hmm?" I pop up and wipe the side of my mouth.

"Come go in your bed."

I rub my eyes and say, "Okay, Daddy. I just need to shut down the computer."

"Okay. Good night."

"Good night."

I wait to hear the sound of his bedroom door close before I turn the monitor back on.

```
Appletini: agqqqqqqqqqqqqbcagagetwhsdw
   r-p;l
Appletini: m,\]4..e///r
Appletini: 6
Multi-Mil: ?
Multi-Mil: u there?
```

Ugh. That's what I get for leaning too hard on the keyboard.

```
Appletini: sorry about that
Appletini: it was an accident
Multi-Mil: no prob
Appletini: it was nice talking to you
   but I gotta sign off now.
Multi-Mil: aight sweetness. We'll link
   up soon.
Appletini: ok. Bye.
Multi-Mil: L8R.
```

Chapter 7

"Martine, time for school."

I hear the door close behind my mother, and that's it. Where's my song? I sit up as the shock of it hits me. Even when she and Beresford go on vacation, she still calls and sings to me. She's been doing it for so long that I kind of took it for granted. If she's mad enough to skip my song, she might bring the hammer down on me later.

I start thinking about Greg, and the smile from last night returns. But then reality sets in. What am I going to wear?! I mope my way into the bathroom and shower in the dark. One of those new dresses would do the trick, but there's no use thinking about things that I can't have. I press my forehead against the wall and pray that an outfit will just come oozing out of the showerhead. Beresford knocks on the door a few times to remind me that he still has to pay the water bill. The last knock made the walls shake.

I come out of the shower and head straight for my closet. It feels more like a death march, like I'm walking to the electric chair. I open the closet door, silently hoping that the bag of clothes is still in there. My mother must've moved them when I was in the bathroom. Not like I would've worn them anyway.

I sigh, disappointed, and drop onto my bed. I knew that I was forbidden to wear the new clothes, but now I'm forced to make a decision. I take out my cornrows and put my hair in a ponytail. It looks nice because it has this kinky, wavy thing going on. Even so, how am I going to keep Greg interested if I'm wearing button-down shirts and Gap khakis?

Sulking on the edge of my bed, I notice a box sitting on my desk. There's a note on top of it.

> Martine,
> Sometimes it's what you don't show that's sexy.
> Mummy
> P.S. We still need to talk, young lady!

Inside the box are three velour sweat suits. Even though I know a punishment is coming, I can't help but smile and wonder how my mother knew that these things were in style. Funny, if Cherise hadn't pointed one out to me at the mall, I wouldn't have known myself. They don't have any tags on them, so I'm assuming they are some of her old clothes. Thank God my mother takes care of everything she buys. These things look almost new. She says that fashion goes in cycles so she doesn't throw much of her stuff away.

To say the velour suit fits perfectly would be an understatement. I'll ask her if I can dig through some of her boxes in the attic. I'm bound to find some more nice stuff up there.

"I'm feeling that velour! Where'd you get it?" Cherise seems impressed when I see her in the subway.

"My mother gave it to me. I decided not to wear one of the things we bought from the mall."

I practiced saying that line over and over on the walk to the train. Of course it didn't come out right. Maybe I should've waited until she actually *asked* me about the clothes we bought yesterday before I said anything. Cherise's face is full of doubt as she hears my excuse. She sees through me like I'm a pane of glass. I tell her what happened when I got home yesterday, and she almost flips.

"Damn, Teenie, I swear. You so stupid sometimes. Why you had to tell her I bought them for you?"

"What was I supposed to say? I'm sorry."

"I don't know. Why you ain't tell her you saved up your money or something?"

I shrug my shoulders.

"What did she do with the clothes?"

I look away and don't answer.

"Ugh." She shakes her head and sucks her teeth. "You're the worst!"

I keep quiet for a while, hoping she'll get over it, and give her a Claritin as a peace offering. She takes it and stares at me for a little longer, then changes the subject.

"He never showed up," she sighs.

"Who?"

"You see how you stay? Get a little attention from a boy and totally forget about your friends."

"Oh! Big Daddy. What happened?"

"Did I tell you I was meeting with Big Daddy?"

"No."

"So stop making assumptions then."

"So if it wasn't him, then who were you supposed to meet?"

"Do you want to hear the story or not?"

"Fine. Go ahead."

"I was supposed to meet *him* at Penn Station. You know that waiting area with all the chairs?"

"By the escalators?"

"Yup. I was sitting there for like a hour. I didn't see him, so I just went back home."

"Your mother didn't say nothing when you came in so late?"

She sucks her teeth again. "She wasn't even there when I got home. Braxton must've come for her."

"Well, how do you know she didn't check on you before she left?"

"She didn't."

"But how do you know? Couldn't she have opened your bedroom door and seen that you weren't there?"

"Did I get in trouble?"

"No. I don't think so."

"Well, I guess she didn't check, huh?" She shakes her head and goes back to her story. "Like I was saying, when I got home, I logged on to IM, and he was waiting for me, talking 'bout how he got stuck in the library studying and lost track of the time."

"Library?" I reach out and touch Cherise's forehead to check for a fever. "You alright? It ain't like you to go for the smart ones."

"Shut up. He could be as smart as he wants. He looks good AND he got money."

Now that's the Cherise I know and love. But still . . . "Maybe I should go with you the next time you see him."

The look on her face says it all. She's right, though. There's no way in hell I'd sneak out of my house in the middle of the night.

Cherise and I linger in the hallway before first period but see no sign of Greg. A few guys try to talk to me, but I'm getting pretty good at smiling and saying no thank you. When Cherise and I walk into class, Mr. Speight is in the middle of a tirade.

"Only four people passed," he says with disgust, "and only two people got a perfect score."

There are thirty-some-odd students in the class, so that's an abysmal pass-to-fail ratio. As Mr. Speight makes mention of the perfect scores, all thirty-some students look over at me. It doesn't help that Mr. Speight glances in my direction.

Everyone knows I got the ten out of ten. Cherise is most likely the other since she copied all of my answers. I try to tell her to get at least one wrong so things won't look suspicious. The girl never listens.

"I must be a bad teacher, because that quiz was really not that difficult. And question six, come on, people."

During gym, we get stuck inside on the eighth floor. It's overcast outside and the teacher doesn't want to risk getting caught in a downpour. The rest of the girls are playing volleyball. I hate volleyball, so I convince Cherise to shoot hoops with me at the other end of the gym.

"Spread your fingertips out on the ball and leave a little space between the ball and the palm of your hand. Don't forget to keep your elbow in." I don't even know why I'm wasting my breath, because Cherise uncorks a heave that would have made a shot-putter proud. I feel sorry for the backboard after her shot ricochets to the other side of the court. I chase the ball down, apologizing to the other girls for interrupting their stupid volleyball game, and show Cherise how it's done.

Cherise is shaking her head after watching me hit jump shots from all over the court. "That's just ridiculous, Teenie. No girl should be able to shoot like that."

"And why the hell not?"

She thinks for a few seconds. "They just shouldn't, that's all."

"Don't hate, congratulate," I say just as I flick up another jumper. It misses badly.

"That's what you get for talking crap. I'm going to play volleyball."

Cherise runs over to the other side of the gym and leaves me to work on my form. If there's one benefit to having two older brothers, it's learning how to shoot a basketball. Wazi and Kari had me shooting on a ten-foot rim when I was five years old. Basketball is a big deal in my house. Beresford is a big Knicks fan, and my brothers play on the basketball team at the University of Maryland.

With my jump shot, I'm more than good enough to be on the girls' team, but I have too much going on this year. Maybe I'll try out next year if I'm not in Spain.

Beresford was disappointed, but not nearly as much as the gym teacher, who's watching me drain my seventh foul shot in a row. He's also the girls' basketball coach and he has made repeated attempts to get me to join the team. When I asked him if I could shoot at the other end of the gym, he basically ran into his office to get me a ball.

"Martine."

Someone's whispering at the door. I've seen too many horror movies to go skipping over, only to get chopped into little pieces. When I hear my name called again, I lean over as far as I can to the left, cocking my head to get a better angle on the slight opening in the door. I feel even worse when the door opens wider and I can see who's calling me. It's Greg.

He peeks in to see where the teacher is, then fixes his eyes on me, smiles, waves me over. He wants me to step outside of the gym. I look over my shoulder and see that my teacher's distracted, trying to get between two girls who are arguing. I slip out and join him in the hallway.

"What's up, Shorty?"

He opens his arms to hug me. He gives some serious love with his hugs, the kind that makes me feel all warm and mushy inside. I almost don't want to let go, but if I don't, I might faint, because this boy's cologne is making me light-headed. I blink rapidly when he lets go, trying to keep my cool. He steps back so we can talk but holds on to my hand, rubbing the top of it with his thumb. I take in what he is wearing and notice that his lime green zip-up hoodie is open. Underneath, he has on a Bob Marley T-shirt hanging over a light pair of jeans. His sneakers match the hoodie perfectly. "How did you know I had gym this period?"

"I have my ways." He winks and smiles. His smile is so sexy. "I work in the principal's office, so I pulled up your schedule. This is my lunch period—I just wanted to come up and say what's up."

"Okay." My heart is racing right now. After last night's conversation on IM, I can barely make eye contact with him.

"I see you gotta nice li'l jump shot."

I smile. "Yeah, it's okay."

"Where'd you learn to shoot like that? Your dad teach you?"

I nod my head and smile. Why did I answer yes? My dad was a soccer player and couldn't hit the side of a barn with a basketball. It's too late for me to tell the truth, because Greg looks through the gym door and changes the subject.

"So you got Mr. S.?"

I have no idea whom or what he's talking about.

"Mr. S., Mr. Scarinbolasaster," he says, referring to my gym teacher.

"Oh yeah, Mr. S." I smile, nod my head, try to play it off. Scarinbolasaster, that's some name. He licks his lips, and I turn my eyes to a sign showing the fire safety route. I've never paid attention to it before, but my neck is burning up, and I may just have to evacuate.

"I can't stand that dude." Anger flashes across his face but he blinks it away. "So you coming to the game later?"

"The game?"

"Yeah . . . the play-offs . . . ?"

He's looking at me like I'm supposed to know. . . . "Oh! The play-off game." I'm such a loser. I knew all about the game. There are signs plastered all over school announcing it. The local newspapers say we don't have a chance in hell to beat Grady. God, I am so nervous. He smells so good that I'm having a hard time concentrating. "Yeah, I'll be there."

"I know the newspapers say we're gonna get waxed, so we need all the support we can get."

"What time does the game start?"

"Four-thirty."

"Okay." I knew that. Why am I asking such retarded questions? He senses it, and after a few awkward seconds, he says, "Aight then. I'll holla at you later."

"Okay, bye."

We hug again and I turn to walk away but he doesn't let go of my hand. He pulls in close and kisses me. A wave of heat rushes through my body. I've played spin the bottle and truth or dare, but this is the first kiss where I actually wanted to kiss the guy. I never imagined that lips could feel that soft. He steps back and smiles, as if admiring his work, before he pushes through the door to the stairwell. I can still smell him after he walks away.

I must've held my breath for the entire kiss, because when that door shuts, I find myself gasping for air. My head is spinning and I start to get woozy. I stumble back toward the wall and slide down. There's a tingling in my tummy, something I've never experienced before. I need to get some air because the heat in my belly is spreading all throughout my body. I don't know what's happening. A smile breaks out on my face, something like that dumb smile Cherise gets.

The door to the gym swings open and bangs against the wall. The noise startles me, and I leap to my feet.

"Are you okay, young lady?"

Considering that Mr. Scarin-whatever caught me sprawled on the floor with a drunken glaze on my face, it's a fair question. There's nothing I can say really. I breeze past him and run back to the basketball, sink another ten in a row.

Chapter 8

"Teenie kissed Greg!" Cherise broadcasts the breaking news to the crew at the lunch table. I kick her in the heel for having such a big mouth, even though I'm grinning from ear to ear.

"Which Greg?"

"The one on the basketball team?"

The first question was from Tamara and the second was from Malika. Cherise takes center stage like she's the one who kissed him.

"Yup. He tongued her down in the hallway during gym class."

"No he did not!" I say, trying my best not to giggle.

"Yeah, okay." Cherise is laying it on thick. I start laughing when she says, "Y'all should have seen her face when she came back in, smiling like she hit the lotto."

"It was nothing big really." Even Sabrina is happy for me, smiling and laughing while she rubs cocoa butter on the back of her feet.

"Greg Millons?" Crystal asks for clarification.

I nod my head and take questions from the peanut gallery. They want a full, step-by-step account of the day's event.

"Well, can he kiss?"

"Yes."

"Did he try anything else?"

"No, he was a gentleman." I probably wouldn't have minded if he wasn't.

"What if he has a girlfriend?"

That's Crystal again. She must have been gulping the Haterade today, because she's the only one not smiling.

"So what?" Cherise jumps in. "If he does, she need to watch her man."

The other girls laugh and then start asking a bunch more questions. Some of the questions are X-rated and I find myself blushing and laughing and saying, "No I did not!" This is two days in a row I've been the center of attention. I could get used to this.

"Where's the fire?" Tamara asks as we see a bunch of students, mostly girls, running toward the center section of the lunchroom.

Cherise grabs my arm and yanks me up from the table. "They're putting up the results of the cheerleading tryouts."

"Why are we looking if you know you already made the first cut?"

She shushes me. "The head girl winked at me, dummy. It's not official yet. Besides"—she leans in closer—"I want to see who the competition is."

There's a big crowd forming near the wall as a whole bunch of girls fight to get closer to the list. I notice a woman posting something on the other side of the lunchroom. I don't even have a chance to think about checking to see what she's doing. Cherise yanks my arm so hard toward the cheerleader list that I almost catch whiplash.

Cherise forces her way in front of the list and starts looking for her name.

"What the hell? How are you supposed to read this?" She's annoyed because they have the results listed only showing the last five digits of everyone's Social Security number. "How the hell am I supposed to find myself here? I don't know my Social—"

"There you are." Only God knows why I know her SS number.

"Oh." She smiles for a split second, then frowns. "Well, how come my name's not on top?"

"They probably have it ordered alphabetically but only show your SS number so—"

Before I can finish speaking, Sohmi and Sabrina let out ear-piercing shrieks. I guess that means they made round two. Cherise goes over and gives them high fives.

"I don't get it."

"Me either."

Malika and Tamara are shaking their heads and talking about Cherise, Sabrina, and Sohmi.

"I don't understand what the big deal is. It's not even like they're real athletes."

"I know, right? What do you think, Teenie?"

"Uh-huh." I hardly hear a word of what they're saying because my attention is focused on the other side of the room. I think I heard Tamara say she wanted to join the football team. She has got to be crazy.

I wasn't sure before but now I know that's the list I've been waiting for for three months. I recognize two girls who were sitting near me during a YSSAP info session. One of them is trying to contain her own happiness while she does her best to keep her friend from crying.

"Do you know those girls?"

I didn't realize Cherise was standing next to me. I shake my head at her question and say, "No, I don't know them." Sabrina and the rest of the crew start walking back to the table.

"Okay. So . . . why're you staring over there so hard?"

"I think that's the list for that program."

"Oh! The one to Spain?"

"Yup." Wow, she actually remembered.

"Mmm. Girl, you're so lucky to be going. There are going to be a ton of cute Spanish boys, and you know how I love me some Spanish boys."

"Not that kind of Spanish, Cherise." I won't even lie. When I was younger, I thought everyone that spoke Spanish was caramel-colored and from Puerto Rico. They all just got lumped together as Spanish people. "And I don't even know if I got in yet."

"So why are we standing over here?"

My fingers have been crossed so hard that the tips are starting to turn purple. Cherise nudges me a little, encouraging me to go look at the list. I've waited a long time for this moment and now that it's here, I'm not so sure I want to know the results.

"Come on, Teenie. Hurry up. I gotta pee."

Cherise always comes up with the most eloquent ways to motivate me. With that, we finally walk over to the list.

Cherise asks, "Do you see your name—I mean—number?"

I've scanned the list four or five times. It's not there. I can't believe it. "No." I worked so hard and I didn't get it.

"Youuuuu didn't make it?"

I shake my head. What did I do wrong? My grades were good enough. I've never worked so hard in my life.

"We're going to that office, because that has to be some kind of mistake."

"No, Cherise, it's okay. My name is not there. I didn't make it."

"No, it's *not* okay, Teenie. We've been looking forward to this for months." We? All this time I thought she didn't want me to go. "There's no way you're not going."

"But what else can I do? I didn't get it." My eyes are starting to tear up.

"Well, first thing you're gonna do is stop that damn crying. We need to go talk to somebody about it."

"How're we going to do that?" I wipe my face. "We can't just walk out of the lunchroom."

"Leave that to me. Let's go get our bags."

We grab our bags and walk to one of the exits. There are two attendants guarding the door. "Cherise, let's just forget it. We can go later."

"Later when? The basketball game is today."

"But how are we going to get out?" I've just watched the door monitors turn back like four students as Cherise and I get closer to the door.

"I *said* leave that to me."

By the time we reach the exit, Cherise is hunched over and leaning on me for support. She lifts her head to the door monitor and in her most desperate voice forces out the word "cramps."

The door monitor's reaction is immediate. He jumps up from his chair and runs over to the elevator to push the button. I thank him as the elevator closes and Cherise stands up and looks at me, saying, "I'm the best."

"Yeah, yeah."

"Can I help you?"

We're in the study abroad office and I go to open my mouth but Cherise takes charge. "Yes. I want someone to tell me why my friend didn't get the foreign exchange program."

"Do you mean the study abroad program?"

"Same thing."

The girl does not look amused by Cherise's tone and

aggressiveness. "Well, actually, they're different, and for your information, anyone can participate in the program as long as they pay the cost. Are you talking about the scholarship?"

"Yes. That's what I meant."

"Well, YSSAP has very strict criteria for who gets scholarships. It sounds like your friend didn't make the cut." The girl has a smug grin on her face while she looks me over.

"Okay, Ms."—Cherise pauses to read her nameplate—"Azalia Quinones. Are you the person who makes the decisions as to who gets the scholarships?"

"No. But I—"

"Didn't think so. Can I speak to someone who knows what they're talking about, please?"

Azalia's mouth drops the same as mine. Before she has a chance to give Cherise a piece of her mind, Greg walks in from next door and puts his hand on her shoulder. She melts, much like Cherise and I do when we see him. He smiles and says, "These two in here giving you trouble, Azalia?" He pronounces her name the Spanish way, not "Azayleah" like Cherise and I thought it was.

She's grinning from ear to ear and says, "Nothing I can't handle," then turns to Cherise and gives her a stink look, adding, "But this one here has a smart mouth."

I can see Cherise's blood boiling, but surprisingly, she bites her tongue. Maybe for once she realizes that it's not about her. Cherise is keeping quiet but she is locked in a staring match with Azalia, and I'm not so sure she'll win this one. Greg picks up on it and tries to keep things from escalating.

"Why don't you let me take care of this? Matter of fact, can you do me a favor? Can you get me a Red Bull from the bodega? I want a little boost for the game later." He pulls a twenty from his money clip and says, "Get something for yourself too."

Azalia giggles and says, "Thank you," falling all over herself, trying to look cute.

Okay, girl, take it easy and stop trying so hard. Can't she see that Greg's not even paying attention to her? She gives Cherise one last dirty look and walks out of the office.

"What's up, Teenie? How you doing, Cherise?"

"Hi, Greg," we both say at the same time.

"You work here too?" I ask.

"I work everywhere. I run this school, Shorty," he says, smiling and winking.

Cherise and I both laugh.

"So what can I help you ladies with?"

Cherise pinches the hell out of my back to get me to keep talking. "Oww . . . I applied for the YSSAP scholarship but I didn't get it. We came down here to see if there was anything I could do or if they made a mistake or something."

"Yo, I don't blame you for going after that scholarship. That program costs like twelve grand or something."

Cherise's eyes open wide when she hears the amount. Besides the momentary lapse, she does a good job of hiding her surprise.

"Hmm." Greg pushes back in his chair to check if anyone is watching him before leaning forward and saying, "You know, I'm not supposed to be doing this, but let's see what the deal is." He's pitter-pattering away on the keyboard, but his hand placement is way off. No wonder he was so slow typing yesterday. "Wow. Your grades are pretty good."

"Thanks." Since his eyes are going from the keyboard to the computer screen, I take the opportunity to examine every inch of his face. I don't see one pimple anywhere, and the line of his haircut looks like it was done with a ruler and razor blade. Cherise elbows me and gives me a funny face, telling me to stop staring.

After a little more typing, he says, "Oh, okay. I see what the problem is. It says here that you fell a little short on your community service requirement."

I look at Cherise. She shrugs her shoulders because she knows what I'm thinking, that I would've been a shoe-in if she didn't talk me out of volunteering at the hospital last semester. I can still hear her saying, *No one pays attention to that stuff.*

"I can't add you directly to the program itself, but I can put you on sort of a waiting list. You'd have to get your average up one point to qualify. You think you could do that?"

"I can try."

"Yes. She can do it." Cherise looks at me, more than a little annoyed.

"Okay. I've done all I can. It's up to you now." He's smiling.

"Thank you."

"Y'all coming to the game, right?"

I smile while Cherise responds, "For sure. We'll be there."

"Alright. Excuse me. I gotta get outta here." He looks at

the clock and says, "Where is this girl with my Red Bull?" as he walks out of the office.

Cherise takes her hand and starts fanning both of us. "That boy is hot!"

My feet don't touch the ground for the rest of the school day. I feel like I'm floating. *The* hottest boy in the entire school kissed me *and* did me a huge favor and put qualifying for that scholarship back in my hands. I always imagined what my first real kiss would feel like. My dreams were nowhere close to the real thing.

"Teenie, don't you hear me calling you?"

"Hmm?"

"Can you please pass me the forceps?"

"The what?"

Garth points to them, and I pass them over. We're supposed to be dissecting a male bullfrog in bio lab, but I haven't really been much help. He's going for extra credit, trying to remove the pituitary gland. I am still thinking about Greg, replaying that beautiful scene again and again in my head. Damn, that boy is fine.

"Can you hand me the scalpel?" I hand it to him. "The scalpel, please."

"I gave it to y— Oh, sorry." I had passed him a pencil. I take it back and hand him the scalpel. He looks at me funny and shakes his head before getting back to his incision.

I have got to be the luckiest girl in the world. Normally, the only time good-looking guys talk to me is to get Cherise's number or my English homework. But now things are different.

The best-looking boy in the entire school is after me. Who knows where this could lead. I might be getting a little ahead of myself, but Martine Millons definitely has a nice ring to it.

"Teenie."

"Yes, Garth?" Why does he keep bothering me today?

"Are you okay?"

"I'm fine. Why wouldn't I be?"

"Because you're leaning on the desk and there's formaldehyde all over it."

I jump back and glance down at my jacket. My sleeve is dripping with frog juice.

"I suggest you put some baking soda on that. Formaldehyde does not agree with that sort of fabric."

It takes me almost fifteen minutes to scrub the formalde-funk out of my jacket. By the time I get back from the bathroom, Garth has finished the dissection and cleaned up what was left of the specimen. He even took the time to pack up my book bag.

"I got the pituitary out. It wasn't the cleanest cut."

"Oh, come on, Garth. I'm sure it was fine."

The bell rings, and we walk out into the hallway with the rest of the class.

"I saw the YSSAP list up. . . ."

"I didn't make it." Garth's shoulders sag before I get a chance to say, "I got put on a waiting list. I have to raise my average a point to qualify. I hope I can do it."

"I wouldn't worry so much about raising your average."

"I have a math test coming up. If I knew it would be this important, I would've started studying for it like a month ago."

"Don't worry about the math test. I'll help you with that."

"Okay. But I still gotta convince my dad to let me go."

"You haven't talked to your parents about it yet?"

"I wanted to get the scholarship first. I want to make it as hard as possible for my dad to say no because he ALWAYS says no."

"Why wouldn't he let you go?"

"He always comes up with some stupid excuse."

"Really?"

"Yeah. I'm sure he'll say something like one of his friends knew someone who knew someone that went to Spain and got bitten by a mosquito and caught West Nile virus or something."

"Wow . . . well then, you need to make sure you're prepared."

"How am I going to do that?"

"Practice how the conversation would go with me. I'll be you, you be him."

When we get to the center section on the first floor, I look around for Cherise but don't see her. "Alright, but just until Cherise gets here."

"Hi, Daddy," he says, in a really high-pitched voice.

"I don't sound like that, stupid," I say, and slap his arm.

"I know, I'm just messing with you. Hi, Dad."

"Hey, Martine. Come, let's eat dinner."

"Well, I wanted to talk to you about—"

I signal time-out with my hands to stop him. "See, that

just won't happen. He's not going to hear a word I'm saying if he doesn't get to eat first."

"Point taken. Okay, Dad, I'll fix your plate for you."

I perk up. "Hey, that's not a bad idea."

"Oh, I don't mind at all."

I forgot I'm supposed to be in character. "Thank you, sweetheart."

"So how was your day today?"

I signal time-out again. "That's risky. Once he starts talking, I'll never get a word in."

"So, Daddy, there's something I've been meaning to talk to you about. It's a study abroad opportunity called YSSAP. It's a prestigious program that my school offers to only the top students. I've been accepted on a conditional basis but I—"

"How much does it cost?"

"There's a scholarship—"

"How much does it cost?"

Garth shrugs his shoulders. "Sorry, Teenie. I'm not sure how to answer that one."

"No worries. I gotta go anyway. There's Cherise. I'll let you know how it goes tomorrow."

"Okay. Just tell him about all the things you're going to be doing. I can't see how it won't work," he says with a smile.

Garth walks with me toward her and raises his hand to say hello. Cherise makes him pay for his bravery when she points to the exit door and says, "Keep walkin'!!!"

Garth drops his head and sulks his way to the exit.

"Why'd you do that, Cherise?"

"Sometimes you gotta put people in their place before

they get the wrong idea. Just because me and you is friends don't mean I gotta socialize with nerds."

"You don't have to be so mean to him. He's so nice. He probably just wanted to—"

"Yeah, yeah, whatever. Anyway . . . I'm meeting up with my friend at Penn Station tonight. He said he wants to make up for yesterday."

"Why can't you just keep your butt in the house?"

"Because I made plans and I don't want to stay in the house. What's wrong with me going out?"

"I don't know. I kind of have a bad feeling. Maybe it's like woman's intuition or something."

"Woman's intuition? What the hell do you know about woman's intuition? You're fourteen, Teenie."

"I don't know. I'm just getting a weird feeling."

"Yeah, it's called jealousy."

"Shut up."

"And when did you start giving me advice about boys? Are you serious?"

"No . . . I just want you to be careful, that's all."

"Uh-huh. Don't worry, I will. Let's hurry up and get to the gym before we can't get in."

Okay . . .

Chapter 9

The gymnasium is packed, standing-room-only on the sidelines. We had to sneak in through the boys' locker room because there was a line halfway down the hallway from the gym door. On the way through the locker room, something dawned on me. "Cherise, how do you know your way around this place so well?" Cherise was zipping through there like she had a GPS. She giggled, saying, "Don't ask."

Even though I've been to plenty of Knicks and Liberty games, it still feels great to be so close to the action. This is Tech's first play-off game in years, and a home game at that. Grady is a powerhouse every year but got off to a slow start this season because of injuries.

I see a few of my friends already in the stands. Tamara and

Malika are on the other side of the gym near the door, while Crystal, Sohmi, and Sabrina are in the middle of the bleachers. It looks like they spent some time in front of the bathroom mirror fixing their hair and makeup. I'm about to laugh when I hear the Grady players make their loud entrance. A player on their team yells, "WHOSE HOUSE?" and his teammates respond, "OUR HOUSE!!!" The booing of the crowd drowns them out before they have a chance to repeat the chant. These guys are cocky. Cherise is grinning from ear to ear.

Everyone goes crazy when Greg leads the Engineers into the gym. Designer jeans do him no justice, because he looks even better in his shorts. His legs are muscular, especially his calves. He looks comfortable, confident, like he *knows* he's the man. I try not to stare at him too hard, but I'm not having an easy time of it. God broke the mold after making him.

Both teams are doing their warm-ups before the game starts. Just from the nonchalant way he's shooting his layups, (his "economy of motion," as my dad would say), I can tell that number 21 is Grady's best player. I try to point it out to Cherise, but she's too busy looking at number 3, because "he's cute and has on the new Jordans."

I notice right away that Grady has a bigger team than we do. "Looks like Grady has more size up front than Tech."

"I bet they do," Cherise says, with a dirty grin on her face.

The game starts, and Grady jumps out to an early lead. Grady's players are better than Tech's, but Greg is keeping us in the game. He's scoring from all over the place, and unlike most star players I've seen, he passes the ball to his teammates. Grady tries double-teaming him, to little effect. He is making all the right decisions, playing a great game.

At halftime, Grady is ahead by six.

"I hope we have enough time."

I'm a little surprised to see that Cherise is actually showing some school spirit and taking an interest in the game. "Don't worry. We're only down six. There's still a half to play."

"What? Girl, what you talking about? I hope I have enough time to give number three my phone number when the game is over."

"You're the worst."

When the second half starts, the game gets tighter and the intensity picks up. These are the kinds of games that my dad loves. There are hard fouls, shifts in momentum, everything that makes basketball so much fun to watch. Because of Greg's great play, we only trail by one with the game on the line. We inbound the ball at half-court with nine seconds to go. Greg starts under the basket and springs out to the top of the key when the referee puts the ball in play. He catches the ball at the top of the circle and squares up to the basket. Greg shoos away his teammate who slides over to set a screen for him. He wants all the glory for himself, and he deserves it. There are seven seconds left on the clock. Greg stands still and holds the ball high above his right shoulder. The Grady defender is all over him, not giving him any room to get off one of his beautiful jump shots. Greg smiles at him with three seconds on the clock and takes a jab step left. The defender bites on the move, and Greg drives to his right. He takes two dribbles and pulls up. He pump-fakes, and the Grady defender goes flying past him. Greg elevates for the game winner and lets it go as the buzzer sounds. Everyone in the stands rushes the court after the shot hits nothing but net.

"Come on, Teenie, let's go."

"What? Wait, I want to talk to Greg."

"Nope. Let's go. I gotta be out. I told you I got things to do tonight."

Cherise cuts me off before I can protest again.

"Look over there." She's pointing to the crowd of girls jumping up and down around Greg. "Do you wanna be one of those people we make fun of?" I guess she's right. Those girls look like straight-up groupies, screaming their heads off and trying to touch Greg. "How the hell did Sabrina and Sohmi get over there so fast?"

Cherise read my mind. Sohmi and Sabrina somehow managed to get from the top of the bleachers to within inches of Greg in the blink of an eye. "I guess you're right. I'll wait until later."

"Yeah." She's looking at her watch. "You've already seen him twice today. Just chat with him later, and don't be all pressed either. When he logs on, don't say anything. Let him start the conversation. If he does, then you know he's feeling you."

I nod my head. This is good stuff. I'd better take notes.

"What're you doing? Put that away."

I put my pen and notepad back in my bag and catch Cherise looking at me like she's ready to slap me. She mumbles something under her breath and waits for me to start walking out.

"That was such a nice shot, wasn't it?" I say. Greg's teammates carried him out of the gym on their shoulders.

"Yeah. It went right in like whoosh!"

Like whoosh? It's no wonder Cherise and I don't talk about sports. Now boys, that's another matter altogether. Normally this would be the time where she would be talking about some of the cute guys on the other team or some lummox in the crowd whose underarms smelled like week-old cabbage water. She seems preoccupied. I'd bet my big toe I know exactly what she's thinking about.

"So what're . . . where're you supposed to go later?" Cherise is staring out of the window of the train. The train wheels are screeching while it makes a turn, so she doesn't hear me. "Cherise." I nudge her.

"Huh?"

"I said where are you going later?" She must not have heard every word, because it takes a moment before she responds.

"We're supposed to go to the movies and then he's taking me to dinner."

"Oh."

We pretty much sit in silence for the rest of the train ride. When we get off, Cherise turns to me and says, "I told my mother that I'm staying by you, alright?"

Words aren't needed, because my face spells out I A-M C-O-N-C-E-R-N-E-D.

"Don't gimme that look, Teenie."

"What look."

"That look you always try to give me when you don't want me to do something."

"I just think you're putting yourself in unnecessary danger."

"I'll be fine, don't worry."

"But why do you have to meet him at night again? Don't you think that's kind of strange?"

"Don't worry, Teenie. I *said* I'll be fine, okay?"

Everything's not, but I say okay anyway.

Chapter 10

I once read that the key to a man's heart is through his stomach. Judging from the way my mother cooks, it's no wonder that Beresford is wrapped around her little finger. My mother made a big pot of rice and peas and baked red snapper. Beresford must be drooling all over himself waiting for me to come home. I could smell the food before I even opened the door, and sure enough, once I push my way in, he leaps up from his chair.

"Why you home so late, young lady? I was worried about you."

His growling stomach betrays why he was so worried. "Sorry, Daddy. I was at the basketball game. Gimme five minutes and we can start dinner."

"Okay," he says, holding on to his belly. "Who won the game?" he asks while I jog up the steps.

"We did. Buzzer-beater."

"Nice!"

One thing that Beresford insists on is that we eat as a family. Since my brothers are away at school and my mother works nights, eating as a family is usually dinner for two. The rule about family meals is one of the few things he does that I think make sense. I love my father, but Lord have mercy is he weird. He is as old-fashioned as old-fashioned can be. That dang flattop has been on top of his head since the beginning of time, and he's worn the same cologne (which he baths in) since he first started dating my mother. I don't know if Brut for men was popular back in the day, but the fact that he buys it in CVS should say something. When I asked him about it, he said, "Your mother did like me back then and she still like me now, so I ain't got to change nothing."

I understand that people get set in their ways, but when it comes to some of his rules, they don't make sense at all. I wish someone would explain to me why I have to finish the bottle of apple juice before I can open the carton of fruit punch. And forget taking a drink while I eat. I have to finish all of my food before I can drink any water or juice. I could be eating a sandwich made out of sand and sawdust and Beresford would say, "Eat all yah food first. You gonna fill up yah belly with drink and you ain't gonna leave no room for dee food."

My father's strict rules make me love the times that I've

eaten at Cherise's house. Her mother leaves money and we get Chinese or pizza and sit in front of the TV. I make sure to drink some soda right after my first bite, and we crank the volume on the TV all the way up. The only time Beresford lets us eat in front of the television is during the Super Bowl or the NBA finals.

There is a downside to eating at Cherise's house, though. I can count on one hand the times that I've eaten there and her mother ate with us. Cherise tries to play tough and all, like it doesn't bother her. Every now and then she lets her true feelings show, saying I'm lucky. If she thinks I'm lucky, she can trade places and eat dinner with Sir Blabs-a-Lot any time she wants.

As usual, he does most of the talking during dinner, but tonight I have an agenda—that's if I can get a word in. My dad reaches for a plate and moves over to the stove.

"Oh, let me get that for you, Daddy. You had such a long day at work."

I don't have to tell him twice. Garth was right on the money with that suggestion.

Beresford's been going on and on about a new laptop computer his company gave him. He keeps pronouncing it "labtop," no matter how many times I correct him. He's already made me promise about fifty times to help him set it up. Once I promise for the fifty-first time, he goes back over to the table and jumps right into one of his long-winded stories. This one sounds familiar, so I set my responses to autopilot. "For real, Daddy? Wow, that's crazy." Now he'll start talking about how somebody, probably Priscilla, did something wrong and how he had to pick up the slack. I wonder how this lady keeps her job, because according to my dad, she is a waste of brain matter. Here it comes.

"Martine, I tell you that woman is incompetent. She left out the entire section detailing the violations, the most important part of the document. And you know who had to fix she mess?"

Hmm, let me guess. "You had to do it?" My mouth is wide open with shock, to get him to think I actually care.

"That's right. But as soon as you show me how to use that labtop, I'll be able to review her mistakes on the subway."

"*Laptop,* Daddy, *laptop.*"

"It wouldn't surprise me one bit if she was teefin' and robbing the SEC blind."

My dad has these sayings—I call them Beresisms—and "teefin'" is one that he uses most frequently. Teefin', or stealing, is done by a teef (thief) or, when my dad's really angry, a teefah. It's no wonder that growing up I thought Queen Latifah was a criminal mastermind. Lord, this man is strange.

My parents have always made sure to include God in our house. We pray before we eat every meal and go to church every Sunday. My dad usually does the honors. "Lord God, we thank You for this food. Bless the hands that prepared it and make it nourishment to our bodies. In Jesus's blessed name, amen."

When I was four years old, Beresford let Kari say grace, and my brother said, "Rub-a-dub-dub, thanks for the grub." My father sent him to his room, and I had to stuff my mouth full of broccoli to keep from laughing. Wazi got sent to his room too because he couldn't stop smiling. I don't realize I'm smiling about it until Beresford asks, "What's so funny?"

"Oh, nothing. I was just thinking about the game-winner today."

"Hmm," my father grunts as he shovels a spoonful of rice into his mouth. "I read in the papers that Grady had a much stronger team."

"Yeah. They're usually really good, but our best player really played well."

My dad nods his head. "Martine, all the plantain is gone?"

"There's plantain? I didn't see it." He raises his hand to stop me from getting up and says, "I'll get it."

As he stands and walks to the stove, he bumps the edge of the table, and his spoon falls on the floor. To call that thing a spoon is a stretch because Beresford has made some serious alterations to it. When I watch him use it, I think about one of those cheesy infomercials that say, "It slices! It dices!" He calls it his spife—part spoon, part knife—and keeps it in a special box wrapped in an embroidered cloth with his initials on it. He used to just keep it in the cloth, but now he locks it in a box because Kari tried to eat with it when he was little and cut his lip.

It's razor-sharp on one side, and Beresford uses it to cut chunks of steak, chop up vegetables, peel apples, and crack open chicken bones so he can suck out the marrow. Both of my parents suck the mess out of some bones, and I think it's so gross. My dad managed to carve two hooks into the spife so he can eat spaghetti. I don't know how he does it, but he flicks his wrist around and gets a bunch of noodles curled onto it.

My father picks up his prized possession, rinses it off at the sink, and sits back down to eat again. I get up from the table and walk to the stove. "How many do you want, Daddy?"

"What? Oh, the plantain. I forgot—sorry. I'll take four pieces."

I might as well get a little extra gravy while I'm up.

"So how was school today?"

Finally! I've been waiting for him to ask me that. This is probably my best shot to bring up YSSAP. While he was busy talking about Priscilla the Klutz, I've been trying to figure out exactly how to change the subject. "School was great, Daddy. I had a pop quiz in American studies."

"How did you—?"

"A hundred," I say, cutting him off. If I let him start talking again, I'll never get to ask him. "Then later on, in math class, we started going over some new material. And after that, I found out that I'm on a waiting list for YSSAP—it's a program to study abroad for a semester," I say, handing him one of the pamphlets. "All I need to do is raise my average one point and I qualify for a scholarship," I add, because there's no way my dad would pay the regular tuition.

I can feel hope swelling in my chest as he sits and listens to every word without interrupting. He even puts his spife down. I start having visions of fiestas, drinking sangria with my new friends Juan Carlos and Adriana—well, maybe a sip— taking a weekend trip to the beach in Majorca.

"Why Spain?" he asks, revealing the slightest bit of interest maybe?!?!

"It was either Spain or France, and aside from saying *bon-jour,* I don't speak a lick of French."

Beresford is going to let me go. I can feel it!

"The program is all about cultural experience. We would be going on weekly trips to museums, Basque country, and, you ready for this? Here's the best part. You know how you're always saying that the media and history books never show the achievements of black people, right? Well, they're even going to take us to Alhambra, the Moorish fortress in Granada."

He smiles and nods his head as he flips through the brochure.

I've got momentum, so I keep pressing. "It's very afford-able, and I could even chip in and get a little part-time job to help with any spending money I might need."

"Affordable? How much is affordable?"

"Well, there are some expenses that I would be responsi-ble for."

My dad looks down and rubs his head in frustration. He brings his eyes back up and says, "How . . . much . . . does . . . it . . . cost?"

I pause, then blurt, "Thirteen thousand dollars."

"No."

"But, Daddy. I can get a scholarship. I would just need spending money."

"Young lady, have you seen the exchange rate recently?"

"But . . ." He picks his spife back up. That means stop talk-ing. I'll try my luck with my mother in the morning.

• • •

"Oh Lord. My belly gon burst," Beresford says, leaning back in his chair in a glazed stupor.

While I'm putting the food away, all I can think about is going back upstairs to start finding an outfit for tomorrow. I have no choice but to put YSSAP on the back burner until I can speak to my mother about it. It's not like I could talk about it if I wanted to. Beresford is blabbing away full speed again. I feel like stuffing the sponge in his mouth, because I'm sick of the sound of his voice.

My brothers used to watch *Charlie Brown* when we were small. The classroom teacher had this droning voice, like *Wah womp womp womp*. That's what Beresford sounds like today. I usually try to listen a little more when he criticizes Priscilla, the "blasted half a idiot," which in his eyes is ten times worse than being a regular idiot, because then at least you have an excuse. I'm still upset with how quickly he rejected me when I was telling him about Spain, so I see no point in listening to him.

"*Wah womp womp* Priscilla. *Wah womp womp womp*."

"Oh no, that's terrible, Daddy."

"*Wah womp womp* incompetent. *Wah womp womp* half a idiot."

"That sounds like it's really frustrating to deal with."

I can't push the scraps of food into the garbage fast enough. It's my turn to wash the dishes. Hmm, let me see if I can weasel my way out of this. I turn the water on and soap my plate and the serving spoons that are on the counter. Here goes.

"Wah womp womp . . ."

I clutch my stomach and start to groan a little.

"What's wrong, sweetheart?"

"Cramps."

Beresford grabs the dishrag from me as soon as he hears the word. "Oh, oh! Go upstairs and relax. I will take care of the dishes."

Works like a charm.

Chapter 11

Young lady, have you seen the exchange rate recently? I've heard my mother call Beresford a stubborn jackass before, and I couldn't agree with her more. He is so close-minded sometimes. If it's not something he likes, it must not be worth trying. If he had said, "I'm too cheap to pay," I wouldn't be so pissed. How in the world did he bag a hottie like my mother? I hope Greg doesn't get this way when we get older.

    Garth Vader: hey Teenie.

Garth is the only one of my friends on Messenger. I was hoping to get a chance to talk to Greg and congratulate him for his game-winner, but he's not online.

I don't feel like hearing about some new planet that has

evidence of water or how chimps are more closely related to humans than other apes. Matter of fact, I'm getting even more annoyed that I remember him telling me that stuff. I'll talk to him tomorrow.

Garth Vader: you there?

I log off and start looking for an outfit to wear tomorrow. I'm not wearing velour two days in a row, so I'm going to have my work cut out for me if I'm going to impress Greg. How did I ever wear half of this stuff? How many pairs of penny loafers can one person have? Who the hell wears penny loafers anymore anyway? I have the same style of shirt in five different colors, no variety at all.

The TV is on. I have a slim hope that I'll get some inspiration from it. Some of the shows I flip through are total garbage. How they stay on the air is a mystery to me. Anyway, everything these girls have on is tight, and after the tongue-lashing my mother gave me for wearing that Wade dress, that's not a direction I want to go in.

I shut off the TV and walk over to my closet again. The more I think about it, the more I realize I need to go up to the attic, though the thought of it scares the crap out of me. Wazi and Kari told me that our deceased sister Beresforda's ghost haunts the attic. I've watched way too much TV to be messing around with that ghost stuff. Looking at the things on my bed, I know there's got to be a ton more up there. One more glance into my closet, and my curiosity gets the best of me.

• • •

I stand at the bottom of the stairwell leading up to the attic. This must be the one part of the house that no one cleans or fixes. The stairs are all rickety and old-looking, like they lead to the lair of some evil witch. The paint on the wall is chipping. A musty, closed-up smell seems to be coming from the top of the landing. The rusty chain hanging from the light clinks against the wall after I pull it a few times. Of course the stupid thing doesn't work. There are some cobwebs in the corners near the top of the stairs and a thin layer of dust on the banister. When I reach the top of the stairs, I push the door and almost turn around when I hear that creaky sound-of-a-door-opening-in-a-horror-movie noise. I stand still for a while and listen out for any more noises. If I hear anything I don't recognize, I am not waiting around to see what it is. I take a deep breath and paw along the wall until I find the light switch.

When my eyes adjust to the light, I realize that the attic is in much better shape than the staircase. I'd be willing to bet money that my mother has a big say in how things are organized up here. Come to think of it, I can't ever remember seeing my father up here except when he's carrying things up for my mother. He keeps all his tools and crap in the basement. It's actually rather clean and orderly up here, except for that musty smell, kind of like a mix of burnt toast and mothballs.

My mother has her things packed up in boxes, thankfully, with writing on the top detailing what's inside. I push aside the box of miniskirts and drag the one filled with spring shirts back to my room. I go back up to turn the light off and spot a huge wardrobe off in the far corner. It's so big I wonder why I didn't notice it when I first came up the stairs.

This is usually the part in the movie where I am screaming at the screen, trying to tell the character not to go near the closet so the monster can suck out her eyeballs, but I am drawn to this thing the longer I look at it. It just looks so mysterious and full of surprise, like the closet in *The Chronicles of Narnia*. From across the room I can see the detail that went into making the closet. There are small figurines carved into the framework and shiny brass knobs on the drawers. I'm having a hard time understanding why this thing isn't in the hallway. That's before I notice that it's leaning toward one side. When I get closer, I realize that one of its legs is missing.

I open the closet door, still afraid that something might jump out and try to eat me. When I take a good look at what's inside, I smile, because I know I've hit the jackpot. There's a Peg-Board on one of the doors with a ton of costume jewelry, everything from earrings to faux pearl necklaces. A garbage bag full of scarves lies packed away on one of the shelves. On the bottom of the bag, there's a funky, multicolored shawl that is definitely coming downstairs with me. I see a pair of Sergio Valente jeans folded on the top shelf and some Chuck Taylor Converses still in the box. The sneakers look almost new, and the jeans are ripped in all the right places. I start smiling at my haul, until the hairs on my neck stand up when I remember Beresforda. For a split second, I wonder if these clothes are hers, but my brothers said that she weighed like

three hundred and fifty pounds. Still, there's no sense linger-
ing up here any longer than necessary.

I yank at the shawl. It's caught on something. I give one
last good tug, and a pot falls from the top of the closet. I feel
faint when I see a huge crack on the side of it, before realizing
the crack was already there. Looks like someone did a pretty
lousy job trying to glue the thing back together. Considering
how far it fell, I'm really lucky it didn't break.

I reach to pick it up and I try to figure out what it is. It's a
pretty cool-looking vase with a top on it. I pull the top off and
look inside of it. The dust inside is kind of grayish and chalky.
There's writing on the bottom.

RIP BERESFORDA

Oh my God! This is an urn! With ashes! Beresforda's
ashes! I toss the urn onto the top shelf, and luckily it lands on
its base and stays put after a little wobbling. I grab the clothes
and run back downstairs to calm myself down. Oh boy, I forgot
to turn the light off up there. If I leave that thing on, Beresford will have a heart attack. I run up the stairs, flick the light,
and run back to my room.

"Martine. Why you keepin' so much noise up there?"

"Sorry, Daddy."

107

Chapter 12

In the morning, my mother smiles at me as we go over the literature for the YSSAP.

"Only the best students in my school get to participate in this program. Imagine how this is going to look on my record when I start applying for college."

"I think this is a great idea, Martine. This looks like it will be a wonderful experience for you."

"I know, right? They're going to take us to the Prado and the Dalí Theatre-Museum. And look at the pictures of the campus!" This is working out even better than I expected. Madrid and Barcelona, here I come. I'll be taking afternoon siestas and will be fluent in Spanish in no time. Beresford's going down! He's outnumbered on this one, and he knows better than to go against my mother.

"So how does this scholarship thing work?"

"Well, it covers everything but my spending money, and I only need to put my average up one more point, to ninety-four, to qualify for it. The only thing is Daddy. He didn't sound too enthused when I talked to him about it yesterday."

"Don't worry about your father. I'll take care of him. You just worry about getting your average up to ninety-five."

"Ninety-five? No, no. I only need to raise it a point, so that's ninety-four."

My mother looks over at me and repeats it again. "Ninety-five. Your actions have repercussions and, in this case, penalties."

I zone out while she goes on about what a great opportunity the program will be. I don't need to ask her why she's imposing the extra point. It's a shame that I didn't even get to keep the clothes from the mall. Now I get double screwed.

My mother sees me thinking about it and asks, "Do you think that is unreasonable?"

HELL YEAH!! "Uhh, a little."

"First of all, I want you to give Cherise back the money. Where she getting all that money from anyway?"

I frown and shrug my shoulders, hoping she won't press the issue. I zone out. How in the world am I going to raise my average to a ninety-five? I might as well just give it up, because there's no way I can do that.

"Are you listening to me, Martine?"

"Yes, Mommy."

"What did I just say?"

"Uhh . . . I'm sorry. I didn't hear you."

"Pay attention because I'm not going to say this again. I got a card with store credit. You are to give the card to Cherise immediately. Is that clear?"

"Yes, Mommy."

"I don't like this one bit, Martine. I left a message with her mother, and I'm going to get to the bottom of this."

I hope Cherise doesn't get in trouble.

"And since you place such a high value on clothes, how about you do all the laundry and ironing for a month?"

A month, hmm, I better take it. "Okay, that's fine." I'd much rather do that than have to kill myself with the school-work. We agree, but then it feels like someone dumped a bucket of ice-cold water over my head. Now I have to wash Beresford's underwear. Ugh.

Three trains rumble in and out of the station before I give up waiting for Cherise. I would've gotten on the third train if not for a dusty, butter-toothed hobo who kept bothering me for my number. I tried to be nice and say, "No, that's okay" to whatever he was offering. Still, he kept moving closer to me, over-whelming me with his hot-garbage body odor. Cherise would have known exactly how to get rid of him, but as annoying as he was, I just want to know that she's okay.

I get on the fourth train, knowing I'll probably be late for school. I can't believe she stayed out with Big Daddy. Fun or no fun, I'd be way too chicken to take all of that risk. There's so much that could go wrong. What if something *did* go wrong? What kind of friend am I to let her go out that late? It's all my fault for not trying harder to convince her not to go.

• • •

The first fifteen minutes of Mr. Speight's class are pure torture. The things that I'm imagining are happening to Cherise get scarier with each passing second. What if she's hurt, or kidnapped, or lying in the middle of the woods somewhere crying out for help? I should tell someone in case any of those things are really happening.

I let out a huge sigh of relief when she walks into class. There aren't any visible bruises, and when she gives me a quick smile, I start to feel a little better. As soon as Mr. Speight turns around, I pass her a note.

Where were you? Are you okay?

She grabs the note and starts writing. She's writing a lot, and I keep glancing over at her, waiting for her to finish. She reaches over to pass it to me but doesn't see Mr. Speight walking up behind her in the aisle between our desks. He grabs the note from her and throws it in the garbage without breaking stride or sentence.

"Biological warfare at its finest." He's talking about how the Spanish killed thousands of Incans by giving them blankets laced with smallpox.

When the bell rings, I pack my bag and hustle outside. "What happened?" We only have a minute to talk, because our classes are on opposite sides of the building.

"Where's your next class?"

"Oh, come on. Don't make me wait, Cherise."

"I can't mess around with my bio teacher! He fails you if

you're late more than three times, and I have three already. So where's your class?" She's walking and talking, moving in the opposite direction from my next class.

"Fifth floor, other side of the building."

"What?"

"Fifth floor!" Our voices have to get louder and louder as the hallway swells with students.

"Take a bathroom break and meet me in the northwest staircase on the third floor!"

"Okay. I have something to give you, so make sure you come!"

She stops and shouts, "What?"

I pull the store card from my pocket and hold it up.

She smiles, then raises an eyebrow, her face showing confusion. She frowns at me and shakes her head when she realizes that I'm returning the clothes money to her.

I wait five minutes after Spanish class starts, ask for a bathroom break, and run full speed to the stairwell.

"So he stood you up again?"

"Yeah. I wasted two outfits for nothing."

"Well, how come you didn't meet me in the train station this morning?"

"I just got in late and overslept. I like those jeans, Teenie."

"Thanks." Cherise's stamp of approval puts a smile on my face, because I spent all of last night trying to get my clothes just right. I've got on a white wifebeater with a jeans jacket, the Sergio Valente jeans, and the Chuck Taylors. "So did you hear from him at all?"

"On IM. He said he was too nervous to talk to me. He said that he saw me and that I looked really nice in my dress but—"

"Wait, wait, hold up. He saw you? So that means he was there?"

"Yeah, so what?"

"So what? Umm . . . I know you like watching movies and stuff. Think about this for a second. Right now, you and I are in the scene right before the naive girl"—I pause so she understands that she is the naive girl—"gets her skin peeled off."

"Yeah, yeah. Who are you, Steven Spielberg now?"

We both laugh. "Well, I guess that's the end of that, huh?" Cherise will finally come to her senses and realize this guy is bad news. He stood her up twice AND, even worse than that, was watching her like some kind of predator.

My heart starts beating normally until she says, "The end of what? He's gonna take me on a shopping spree after school tomorrow to make up for the past two days."

"Hold up. You're gonna go out to meet him again?"

"Yup. He's taking me to Macy's."

I'm waiting for her to smile so I know she's joking. Please smile, Cherise. I'm still a kid, but now I see why parents beat their children. I wanna kick her in her butt so hard! "What is wrong with you? Aren't you concerned at all about what's going on?"

"I don't wanna hear it, Teenie. He said he was just scared to talk to me, okay?"

"Listen to yourself, Cherise. He's some big college kid. Why the hell would he be scared to talk to you? That just doesn't sound right."

"What're you talking about, Teenie?"

"Are you blind or just stupid? This guy could be dangerous!"

"Please. I've got it under control."

"Yeah, that's what you think. Then before you know it, they try and do all kinds of nasty stuff. He could be a pedophile, Cherise. Can't you see that?"

"A what?"

"A pedophile. A child molester. I've seen a whole bunch of specials about it. They pretend they're someone they're not and then they kidnap you."

"Oh my God. Whatever. Get out my face with that crap. Didn't I tell you to stop stressing me about this?"

This is normally the time when I shut up and fall back in line so Cherise starts talking about something else. ". . . and I spent like twenty minutes trying to iron the wrinkles out of this shirt until I realized that it's supposed to look like this."

"Cherise, this is serious."

"See, this is exactly why I don't like telling you stuff. You're always stressing me about nothing."

We stay quiet for a few seconds. I can't let it go. "This isn't nothing."

"Will you drop it already?"

"I think you're making a mistake. I think—"

"That's your problem. You think too damn much."

"But you're not thinking at all."

"Yeah, whatever. You been acting like Ms. Know-It-All ever since Greg started whispering in your ear."

"It's clear as day, Cherise. These guys pretend they're someone else, buy you a whole bunch of stuff—"

"So *that's* what it is." She's smiling and shaking her head. "You're mad 'cause nobody ain't buying you stuff."

"Shut up. That's not true, and you know it."

"It *is* true. I know you heated that your mother took those clothes from you. I'd be mad too if I had to wear the stuff in your closet. You been dressing aight the last few days but you can only dig through your mother's boxes for so long."

"Why you gotta be so mean?"

"'Cause you messing up my image. I feel like I've out-grown you."

"Outgrown me? What are you—?"

"You're like deadweight and I'm tired of carrying you. You ain't bringing nothing to the table."

"You're joking, right?"

"Tell me, what do I get outta being friends with you? I always gotta be showing you what to do and telling you what to say."

"Why you trying to play me like that?"

"You get A's on every test but start sweating whenever a guy comes up to you. The guys you do know are the biggest shribs and wear rocked-over shoes. You spend more money on books than anything else. You know the capital of all fifty-two states but you never know what clothes to buy."

"Fifty! There are FIFTY states in the U.S. and I bet you can't even name ten! What's wrong with being smart? You never say anything about me being smart when you're copying all my answers down during a test. I'd love to see how you did in school if I didn't help you all the damn time. Don't come out your face with that crap. You better think about who's carrying who."

"Oh, okay, it's like that? Well, I guess that's that. We'll see who needs who more."

"Cherise, wait. Don't—"

Cherise turns and walks away from me but stops. "Can I have that store card, please?" I reach into my back pocket and hand it to her. "Thank you!" she says, turning to walk away again.

The way she blew up at me, it seems like she'd been thinking about that for a while. I try to hold back the tears, but it's hopeless.

For the rest of the day, the sound of Cherise calling me deadweight rings in my ears like a car alarm. The more I think about it, the sicker I get. I'm upset by what she said, but then I find myself getting more upset at the fact that I let her get me upset in the first place.

The day just zooms by because my thoughts are consumed with that conversation. I've done my best to try and make sure that I don't cross paths with her because I know I'll cry if I see her. Lucky for me she skips gym with a bogus doctor's note. I know I'm feeling bad because they're playing basketball and I'm sitting on the side. I spend my lunch period in the library trying to study for my math test next week. I can barely concentrate for more than a few seconds before my thoughts go back to Cherise.

I don't ever remember Cherise being this mad at me. The worst before today was when I gave Nicholas Bannister her phone number in seventh grade. She only stopped talking to me for an hour back then. Something tells me this one's going to last a little longer.

But doesn't she watch *Dateline* or *Forensic Files* when they talk about stalkers and rapists and stuff? Doesn't she know that Big Daddy has the same profile as the men on those shows? My parents always told me that I should be honest. I thought that's what friends were supposed to do for each other. But what if I'm wrong about Big Daddy? What if he really is a nice guy?

The bell ending eighth period sounds, and my classmates make a mad rush for the door. Markeith Lawson, the kid that sits behind me, knocks my bag over and all my books fall out.

"Hey! Markeith! Hey!"

He turns around and says sorry but keeps running for the door.

What a jerk. I feel like screaming, but I quietly pack my books away. My pen rolled all the way to the radiator on the other side of the room, so I'm the last one out of class when I'm usually one of the first. When I get to the door, I stand aside while the ninth period students barge their way into the room. I'm going to be late for bio, but I don't really care. I just want to go home.

"Teenie, are you okay?"

"Yes, I'm fine." I don't look at Garth when I respond. How could she say those things to me and why do I feel so bad? Why is she so mad at me when I was only trying to help her?

"How did the conversation with your dad go?"

"Fine."

"Is he gonna let you go?"

I say, "I dunno," and flip through the pages of the lab assignment booklet. Since Garth dissected the frog all by himself yesterday, today it's my turn to remove a fetal pig's liver and heart. I think I've read the first page about four times and I still can't figure out what to take out of my tool kit. I can feel Garth watching me intently.

"Are you sure you're okay, Martine?"

"Yes. I'm fine."

"Well, you don't look fine." He pulls the pig from in front of me. I don't protest.

Chapter 13

Whenever my mother feels bad, she throws on *The Best of Sade*. I'm on track 13, and I still feel like crap. All around my room are reminders of my ex–best friend. Any picture I can find of Cherise I stuff into a box and put under my bed, right next to the two teddy bears she gave me for Christmas and my birthday. If I still had the clothes she bought for me, I would burn the hell out of them.

I get tired of sitting in my room, thinking about the girl that was formerly my best friend in the whole world, so I go down to the laundry room and do two loads of clothes. I will finish the whites and delicates on Saturday. I figure I might as well get that stuff out of the way, since I have a term paper due and a big exam coming up next week.

It's not like I can do my schoolwork now anyway. My homework is taking forever to finish. I find myself struggling with questions that I would breeze through if I weren't so distracted. I'll get halfway through a response only to realize that I've answered it all wrong. I'm just about finished when I see Greg log on to his IM. I wait for him to start the conversation, just like Cherise told me. It's almost like I'm talking about someone who died, because I know she'll never speak to me again. As soon as I logged on, she logged off, and probably blocked me in the process. Whatever, who needs her. I block her on my Messenger because I don't want to hear any weak apologies when she comes to her senses.

Multi-Mil: yo Ma what's good?
Appletini: hey Greg. what's up?
Multi-Mil: chillin. Just getting home
    from practice.
Multi-Mil: did you come to the game
    yesterday.
Appletini: yeah I was there.
Appletini: nice shot
Multi-Mil: aight! thanx
Multi-Mil: after that shot, I can
    pretty much write my ticket to any
    school I want
Multi-Mil: I got phone calls from
    like 20 college coaches
    congratulating me.

```
Appletini: that's good
Multi-Mil: u aight? u seem kinda out
  of it.
Appletini: I'm ok.
Appletini: I'm not feeling all that
  great.
```

I shouldn't have said anything to Cherise. I should've kept my big mouth shut, and everything would be fine now.

```
Multi-Mil: oh aight.
Multi-Mil: don't let me hold you up
  then. I'll just catch up with you
  later.
Appletini: you're not mad at me are
  you? ☹
Multi-Mil: nope not at all.
Multi-Mil: you just gotta make it up
  to me tomorrow ☺
Appletini: deal.
Multi-Mil: how bout a blessing
  tomorrow then?
```

A blessing?

```
Appletini: u want a blessing?
Multi-Mil: that would be nice. So what's
  up? u gonna hook a brother up or what?
```

I have no idea what he's talking about but I don't want to seem like a loser. It doesn't sound like much. How bad could it be?

```
Appletini: alright.              .
Multi-Mil: aight then. I'll c u
    tomorrow after school. Meet me
    outside the boys gym at like 4.
Multi-Mil: the team has a little
    walkthrough before our next game.
Appletini: ok.
Multi-Mil: aight sweetie. c u
    tomorrow.
Appletini: k bye.
```

I log off and slump in my chair. I can't figure out what I did wrong today. Am I jealous of what Cherise has with Big Daddy? Maybe a little. No, that can't be the reason I want her to stop seeing him. I just think that she is in serious danger. Why can't she see what I am seeing? I wish my mother were around, because I could find a way to talk to her without ratting out Cherise.

"Martine."

Beresford scares the crap out of me. I'm surprised I didn't hear his feet plodding up the stairs. "Yes, Daddy."

"You finish your homework yet?"

"Just about."

"Good. I want you to show me how to use my labtop again

before dinner. I can't remember how to get to the newspaper site you showed— Wha wrong wit you?"

"Nothing. I was just trying to . . . I just need a nap."

Beresford eyes me for a moment. "I bet that idiot box did burn yah eyeball."

"Hmm" is about all I can muster.

"You sure you alright?"

I nod my head, but my eyes can't lie. My dad might not pay that much attention to me, but he can tell that something has me upset and he's not going to leave until I tell him what it is. He plops down on my desk and waits. I'm trying to think of what to say but I can't come up with anything. This is one of those times where my loyalty to Cherise is being tested. I think she is going to get herself into a world of trouble. Beresford breaks the ice before I can even figure out what to say.

"Look. Does dis have somethin' to do with boys?"

My dad has probably been waiting all my life to have this conversation with me. I overheard him talking to my brothers once and he said something about "you only live once" and "get it all out of your system before you get married." I doubt that he will have the same things to say to me. He sits up in his chair and clears his throat.

"Martine, boys lie. They want dee goodies and they will do and say whatever—"

"Daddy," I cut him off, "Mommy and I had this talk already."

"THANK GOD!" He lets out a huge sigh. "So what's the problem then?"

I hesitate. Once I start talking about Big Daddy, Cherise will never talk to me again, ever. Not like she's talking to me anyway, but I'd rather her be safe and mad at me than end up in "dee ditch by dee road" that Beresford is always talking about. I decide that I'm not going to tell my father unless he guesses.

We sit there for a while, neither one of us saying a word. This would be so much easier if my mother were around.

"Did you and you mother get into a fight? She did look vexed this morning."

I shake my head. She probably was still upset about the bags of clothes.

"You vex with me?"

I shake my head.

"Your brothers do something to you?"

I almost nod my head for all the abuse they put me through, but I shake, grudgingly.

My dad seems out of ideas before the lightbulb goes off in his head and he yells, "Cherise! Something happened to Cherise!" The smile on his face from guessing the right answer disappears when he notices my look of concern. "She in some kind of trouble?"

I nod.

"Something happened with she and she mother?"

Shake.

"She failing school?"

Shake.

"Some boy messing with she?"

The look of concern comes back with a vengeance. My dad gets serious.

"Listen to me, sweetheart. If you don't talk to me, I cannot help you. Tell me what's going on."

I can feel my eyes start to water. My dad takes my hand into his as I try to wipe my tears away.

"Martine. What is it?"

I start crying like a baby and tell him what Cherise is doing.

"Where?"

"Penn Station," I blubber.

Chapter 14

"Do you see her?"

I shake my head at Beresford's question. He was driving like a maniac on the way to Penn Station. It normally takes us about forty-five minutes to get here from our house but my dad made it in thirty. I have never seen him so anxious, with his eyes darting all over the place and his leg shaking so much he can barely sit still.

My dad's been clenching his jaw and cracking his knuckles the whole time we've been sitting down. I probably shouldn't have said anything to him. Who knows how *big* Big Daddy is. What if my dad can't handle him by himself? There are a couple of cops standing near the escalator. I look over at my dad and think about telling him to go ask for help, but I already know better. Beresford wouldn't ask a cop for a piece of bread if he were dying of hunger. He has had tons of bad experiences with police. The one that pops into my head is the time he got a ticket when he was just being a Good Samaritan. Beresford tried to throw away a beer can that was on top of a phone booth, and a cop gave him a ticket for drinking alcohol in public.

I turn my attention away from the cops and look around the packed station. There are people hustling all over the place, and it's hard for me to see much of anything except for bodies zigzagging in front of me. I try to scan as many faces as possible, because I don't want to miss her. I wish Cherise were a tourist because they are the easiest to pick out of the crowds. They don't move with the same purpose that New Yorkers do. They're the people who will walk really slowly, then stop suddenly and look straight up in the air at the ceiling, or the skyscrapers, if they're outside. I've seen more than a few of them get knocked over when they stop like that.

I happen to be focused on a family of tourists when one of them stumbles after being bumped into. Cherise nearly knocks over the mother as she bulls her way through them. She is looking around, and I have to duck my head before she sees me. She spots Beresford before I have a chance to tell him that she's here. She starts backing away but bumps into a man standing near to her.

He's holding flowers in his hand, smiling as he gives them to her. When he reaches his hand out to her, she steps back and her mouth and eyes pop wide open. It's Big Daddy! He's maybe five foot seven, can't weigh more than a hundred and forty pounds. He doesn't look anything like his pictures. He's at least twenty years older than the boy on Facebook.

I'm not sure what a pedophile is supposed to look like, but if I had to describe one, he sure wouldn't look like Big Daddy. How dangerous could he be? He literally looks like he could be a mailman or the guy that takes your ticket at the movie theater. I could just pretend that I don't see them, and Cherise won't get in trouble.

When I look over at my father, I can tell that he hasn't seen her yet. There's something about Big Daddy that seems weird to me. It's not hot at all in the train station, but he's sweating like a whore in church, whatever that means. Plus he has sunglasses on, and my mother told me never to trust a man that wears sunglasses indoors.

I tap my father.

"Hmm?"

Beresford follows my eyes and does a double take when he sees Cherise. There's no way he would've recognized her if I weren't there to point her out. He leaps up from his seat and takes her by the arm. He sits her down and makes a beeline for Big Daddy.

Man, I thought he was mad at Kari and Wazi when they totaled the car, but I've never seen him like this. It's no wonder that Big Daddy turns and starts to walk—no, run—away. My dad goes after him.

They're too far away for me to hear what's going on. Seeing my dad standing across from Big Daddy makes it look like he's in front of a dwarf. Big Daddy is shaking with fear. His head is down and he's nodding and agreeing with whatever my father is saying. Beresford starts to walk away but then he turns back to Big Daddy. I can see my father's mouth moving slowly, and whoa. I think he just said, "If you try to contact her again, I will kill you."

A moment of silence would be noisier than the car ride home. Everyone's eyes are forward and no one is saying a word. It's so tense that I find myself listening to the tires humming over the bumpy FDR Drive.

Before we got into the car, my father pulled Cherise aside for about twenty minutes. She was close to tears and didn't say much while he was talking to her. They sat down in chairs about ten seats away from mine, so I couldn't really make out what was being said. I expected to hear more yelling, at least see my dad's arms flailing while he told her what a dummy she was for endangering her life. I felt sure that he would tell her to come over to me and thank me for saving her. My father didn't do any of that. He sat with her and reassured her that everything was going to be okay. He was holding her hand and had his other hand on her shoulder. The look on his face was more of concern than anger. I hardly ever see Beresford do anything but yell.

Normally I'm not one to try and eavesdrop, but I couldn't understand why she was getting off so easy. I tried not to make it too obvious, but since I was too far to hear, I stole glances at Beresford's mouth, trying to read his lips. What I did manage to pick up from my dad was, "dangerous," "more than you bargained for," and "end up with the witch and a toad." What? A witch and a toad? Oh! In a ditch by the road!

I am trying my best to find anything to take my mind off what's happened tonight. Looking out of the window seems to be my best bet. Beresford glances at me when he notices that I'm staring in his direction but looks away when he sees that I'm looking past him. Nope, I'm not going to think about how I just saved my best friend from being on a milk carton. I'll just look out the window.

I never realized how pretty the East River was at night. When the sun is up, it's easier to see all of the oil and grime that floats on the surface, but at night, with all the buildings lit up, it's actually kind of nice. As long as I stare out the window, I won't wonder why my dad was so nice to Cherise and talks to me like I'm not worth the gum on the bottom of his shoe.

I don't need either of them. They can go fly a kite for all I care. Yeah, I'm not gonna think about it anymore.

My back is turned to Cherise and I can't come up with any good reason why I should turn around. I figure she's going to curse me out sooner or later, so I'll try to keep that from happening for as long as possible. I can't say I feel good about getting her in trouble. Actually, I feel about fifty times worse right now. What if Big Daddy was a nice guy? He didn't look all that threatening. He was just sweating a lot. What if I really ruined a good thing for her?

It is minutes to nine before we pull up in front of Cherise's house.

"Wait here, Martine. I'll be right back."

I had no intention of getting out of the car. I see my father pointing and roll the window down in time to hear him say, ". . . inside and get your mother. I want to speak with her."

Cherise says, "My mother's not home. She went to Cozumel with her boyfriend." Her head is down and her hands are clasped together behind her back. When she's feeling unsure of herself, she does this weird thing with her right foot where she rocks it back and forth on its side. She must really be scared, because she is doing that foot thing nonstop.

My dad tells her, "You're staying with us tonight, so go upstairs and get a change of clothes. I'll speak with her when she gets back."

What? Why the hell is she staying with us tonight? I want to protest, but I don't think my father is open to negotiations. Cherise nods her head and goes into the house. My dad walks back to the car but stays outside, leaning on the hood. He is shaking his head and sighing. I'm still waiting for him to just go off on her. It seems kind of unfair, because I would never have heard the end of it if I tried to pull some crap like Cherise did. He looks like he's about to cry, but when he sees me looking at him, he straightens up and turns his face. My father would smile after stepping on a nail before he showed any sign of weakness.

Cherise comes back downstairs wearing a long-sleeve T-shirt, some pajama pants, and her hair wrapped up in a head scarf. She jammed her clothes into a couple of grocery bags and has her jacket tied around her waist.

When my dad starts the car, I reach for the knob on the radio. I'm getting antsy, and the thought of having to sit in the car without any conversation for ten more minutes is making my head hurt. Beresford glares at me, and I switch it off before he says anything. I figure that any little thing might set him off, and I don't want to be the one who gets the worst of it.

Cherise and I sit at the kitchen table while Beresford warms up the leftovers. Cherise says she's not hungry—but that doesn't stop my dad from setting a place for her. While he's fixing the food, I finally get the courage to look up at Cherise. When our eyes meet, I look away long before she does, because if looks could kill, my heart would've stopped beating.

Before today, I never realized how annoying the sound of Beresford's spife clinking against a plate was. I haven't eaten any of my food and it's probably ice-cold by now. I can't take it anymore. "May I be excused?"

"No." My dad doesn't look up from chopping a chunk of fish. He finishes his food and takes a long drink of his Guinness stout. "How long has this been going on?"

Neither Cherise nor I answer. I look over at Cherise and she still has that mean look on her face, but she is staring down at the floor, shaking her head.

"I *said* how long has this been going on?" The anger in my dad's voice startles me.

"Umm. I . . . I've known him for about three months." I'm surprised that Cherise answered. He wasn't getting a peep out of me.

"Three months?! Three flippin' months?!?!? And you knew about this and didn't say anything?" He's looking right at me. "I am really disappointed in both of you."

"Me?! What did I do, Daddy?"

"Accessory to the fact. You knew what was going on and did nothing to stop it."

"But I told her not to—"

"Shut your blasted mouth. I don't want to hear any excuses."

That kind of talk is usually reserved for my brothers, and now I see why it works so well on them.

"This is very serious. I don't think you two realize the danger that you put yourselves in. You should not be associating with people like that if you don't know them, agreeing to meet them all times of the night. As for you, young lady"—his eyes and finger are pointed directly at me—"how could you call yourself she friend and not stop she from doing this foolishness? Or come and tell me at least?"

Beresford's Bajan accent is coming out in full force. He's all set to give me the third degree when the phone rings. It must be my mother, because his face relaxes a little when he answers it. He leaves the room to talk in private. I play with my rice, sensing Cherise is waiting for me to look up. When I do look up, she rolls her eyes at me as hard as she can. I can't believe she sat there looking at me for that long just to do that. After a few minutes, Beresford comes back into the room and puts the cordless back on the hook.

"Both of you go upstairs and get ready for bed."

When we reach the top of the stairs, Cherise turns to me and says, "Don't you ever in your life even think about talking to me again."

chapter 15

In the morning, I hear my mother's melody. I sit up in the bed and smile, waiting for her to push my door and make everything better. It takes me a few seconds to realize that this morning her song is not meant for me. Her voice trails off as I hear her walk past my room and into the twins' room to sing to Cherise. First I get dumped by my best friend and told never to speak to her again. Then my dad says he's disappointed in me. Now my mother is turning on me too? How is this fair?

When my mother comes into my room, I'm not sure how to react. She starts to sing but then realizes that I am already awake.

"Good morning, sweetheart."

"Morning, Mommy." I guess my mother is done talking to Cherise, because I hear Cherise shuffling into the bathroom.

"How're you feeling this morning?"

"I'm alright."

"Hmm." She nods her head and frowns a little. "I heard about what happened last night." My mother starts stroking my hair and lifts my chin so I will look at her. "You did the right thing, Martine."

"Yeah, right. Tell that to Cherise. She told me never to talk to her again."

"She's angry and can't see past that. Give her some time. She'll see how lucky she is to have you as a friend."

"Maybe I shouldn't have said anything. Then she wouldn't be mad at me. I just want things to be how they were before."

"Things won't ever be the same, Martine, and if you want to become the best person you can be, you will never want things to be the same."

That's not what I was expecting to hear, and my mother sees the look of confusion on my face.

"The only constant in life is change. The sooner you understand that, the easier it will be for you to cope with hard times, learn from them, and grow."

I nod my head as she continues.

"Is this where she got the money for those clothes?"

"Yes."

"The first thing you have to do is forgive yourself. I know that's hard, but you were being a true friend. Cherise will come to her senses one day. If she doesn't, that's her loss." My mother kisses my forehead and leaves me with that one.

I turn the light on in my closet and decide to go with one of the velour suits my mother gave me. There's a small hole on

135

the waistband, barely noticeable as long as I keep the jacket zipped and pulled down over it. I don't feel like ironing this morning, so I carry the suit to the bathroom, hoping the steam from the shower will take out some of the wrinkles.

The water stopped running about ten minutes ago, so I'm pretty sure Cherise is out of the bathroom. As I raise my hand to open the door, she pulls it open. We startle each other before her eyes fall right onto the hole in my pants. She cracks a smile and laughs as she pushes past me.

If this morning is any indication of how things will be between Cherise and me, I had better start looking for a new best friend. I have to keep repeating "her loss" to myself every time she rejects my efforts to patch things up. We leave the house together but she sits on the other side of the train. That's fine, her loss. I'll have more room and won't have to worry about her sneezing on me. Her eyes are so red it looks like she just finished taking a bong hit.

When we get to class, she asks Mr. Speight if she could move to another desk, saying there was gum on hers. Hey, again, no problem, her loss. Mr. Speight sprung another quiz on us this morning, and I know her lazy behind didn't study for it. I hope she gets them all wrong and ends up with a big fat zero.

As tough as I try to play, I still want to talk to squash things with her. Every time I get anywhere near her during gym, she walks away from me. But I don't give up. I need to talk to her, about making up, about Greg and the blessing thing. Finally, I get an opportunity when she bends down to tie her shoelaces as we're walking back into the building after gym class. I jog over and catch up to her. When I stop in front of her, she says, "Keep it moving" without even looking up at me.

"But, Cherise—"

"Get out my face." She finishes tying her shoelaces and walks away.

Okay, now she's starting to get me mad. I understand that she's upset, but I was only trying to help her. If she can't see that, then my mother is right. It is her loss! She's lucky there are five people standing between us on the way up the stairs because all I can think about is how hard she would hit her head on the bottom step if I could reach her collar. If anything, I should be the one that's upset. There's no way my parents are going to let me go to Spain after what she got herself into. Besides being the ultimate cheapskate, Beresford is already super-overprotective of me. I'm sure he thinks that Cherise has corrupted me with her sneaky ways.

"Hey, sweetie."

I almost bump into Greg on my way out of the staircase. He slides his hand around my waist and rests it just above my butt.

"Hi, Greg." My stomach is churning like I'm making butter.

"Everything good with you? You got the crazy Ms. *I'm-'Bout-to-Swing-on-Somebody* look on your face."

"I'm okay. I was just thinking about something."

He eyes me for a second, tilts his head slowly to the side, like he's trying to read my thoughts or something. I'm starting to get uncomfortable with the mind reading when he says, "Oh, alright. Cool. So we still good for later, right?"

Forget feeling uncomfortable. My face probably doesn't show it, but I'm on the verge of a full-scale panic attack. I look up at him, not sure what I should say. He's smiling, so smiling back at him seems like the natural thing to do. His smile gets bigger and he says, "Good. I'll see you at four outside the boys' gym. Don't be late." He winks at me and walks away. I'm lost.

I've spent the last twenty minutes walking up and down the lunchroom looking for Crystal. She's the only one that can help me now. Our table is empty, with everyone but Cherise and Crystal in Quebec. I walk past it and check every corner of the cafeteria. I scope out all the lunch lines, look in the center section, on the other side of the lunchroom, and in the bathroom, but I don't see Crystal anywhere. I'm about to give up when I spot her sitting with some upperclassmen—well, upperclass*women,* in this case. What a relief. They're off in the corner, and as I walk toward them, I can hear some of the girls talking loudly with each other.

"So my mother said I gotta pay my cell phone bill."

"'Cause you got a job?"

"Yup. I was like okay. Mmm-hmm, okay. Puh-leeze. I called Verizon the next day and was like turn that piece of crap off."

While they all laugh, I slide in behind Crystal and tap her left shoulder.

"Hi, Crys."

She turns to look at me and gives a dismissive wave. ILL! What's her problem?

"Listen, Crys, can I talk to you for a second? It's kinda important." I guess I can't take a hint, because she spins around and rolls her eyes at me, like I'm bothering her or something.

"I'm kinda busy right now."

"Oh." I stand there entirely too long before I realize it's time to go. "Alright then, I guess I'll talk with you later." She's already turned her back on me and doesn't say a word.

Embarrassed, I meet eyes with one of the girls sitting with Crystal. Everyone else is sitting at the table looking at me like I'm a loser, but this girl, the pretty one with the nose ring, is burning holes in my pupils. It's been a while since I've felt like a lowly freshman, but the way she looks at me makes it seem like it's the first day of school. As I'm about to turn, she starts smiling at me, though something about her smile doesn't seem friendly. It's almost like she's laughing at an inside joke or something.

"You know, Crystal," the girl says, "you shouldn't be so mean to your little friend. Have a seat . . ." She looks over at Crystal for my name.

"Martine," Crystal responds, with a bit of disgust in her voice.

"Have a seat, Martine."

I'm about to tell her that I can't stay, but her statement was not a request. Crystal puts her bag on the floor, and I slide in next to her.

"So you're friends with my baby cousin?"

"Who? Oh, Crystal. Yeah, we usually eat lunch together." I guess she's Crystal's older cousin.

"Well, any friend of Crystal's is a friend of mine. I'm Passion."

"Nice to meet you."

"Honestly, I have ulterior motives. I wanted to know where you got that sweat suit from. It's hot."

"My mother gave it to me. I'm not sure where she got it, though."

She looks around at her friends and says, "Her mother must have some good taste, huh?" They all laugh. "I really like the color, and it fits you really well."

"Thanks," I say with a smile, thinking my first impression of her might have been off. She seems really nice.

"So do you have a boyfriend, Martine?"

"No."

"Are you seeing anyone? Anyone checking for you?"

"Uhh, no."

"So you're not interested in boys in this school? There are a lot of cuties running around here."

"No. I just kind of stay in my books. That's about it."

"As pretty as you are, trust me, they'll find you."

I fidget and force a smile. The rest of the girls are watching Passion question me like I'm on the witness stand. I think it's time for me to leave. "I have to get going. I have to study for a test I have later."

"Okay. Well, like I said, any friend of Crystal's is a friend of mine, so next time you see me, holla. It was nice to meet you."

"Nice to meet you too." I get up to leave, then I remember why I came over here in the first place. "Oh, Crystal, I need to talk to you real quick."

"What?"

As I'm about to ask her to take a walk with me, Passion says, "Cuzzo, she wants to speak to you in private. Am I right?"

I nod my head and smile nervously.

Crystal gets up from the chair and walks a few feet from the table. "What do you want?"

"Sorry, I don't mean to bother you, I just wanted to ask you a quick question."

"Well, go ahead already, I don't have all day."

"What the hell is your problem? Why you acting so stink?"

"Sorry. I'm just having a rough day."

Her apology feels phony. She's saying she's sorry, but her face tells a different story. I'm desperate, so I ask my question anyway. "Do you know what a blessing is?"

I can tell I have her attention by the way she responds. "A blessing? Someone asked you for a blessing?"

It kind of makes me regret asking her. I try to cover my true intentions. "No, not me. A friend of mine asked me, and I wasn't sure, so I told her I would ask around."

"A friend? Do I know this friend of yours?"

I shake my head.

She looks me up and down like she's trying to read me or something. "Nah. I don't know what it is."

"Okay, thanks." For nothing.

Chapter 16

When my English teacher, Ms. Barney, handed out the syllabus at the beginning of the year, she said it was our responsibility to mark down the day of the exams. She told us that she would not remind us about it and that we should make sure to be prepared for the test. Thank God I already read *Native Son*, because I would've bombed on today's test if I hadn't. Lucky for me, Bigger is one of my all-time favorite characters. The extra-credit questions were easy, so I can get higher than a hundred.

My heart almost skips a beat and the rest of the class groans when Ms. Barney says, "Pens down." No one in the class listens, and they try to sneak in a few more lines before she can waddle down the aisle to grab their essay books. "I said pens down!" she barks.

I'm not upset like the rest of the class is because I didn't have time to finish. I answered both extra-credit questions, and I even had time to review my answers. I'm upset because the bell is about to ring. The test was the only time all day where I haven't thought about Cherise or Greg. Now that it's over, they're both back in my head.

I look up in the front at Sohmi's empty seat. It's almost like God is teasing me. Why of all days is this the day that none of my friends are around? There have been plenty of times when someone has asked me something and I had no idea what the hell they were talking about, only to be bailed out by my clique. It feels like a bad dream, like one of those dreams where no matter what I do, I can't get away from the bad guy chasing me. No matter how many times I turn or twist or change directions, I trip over a tree root and get chopped in the back with a meat cleaver.

As if my encounter with Crystal and staring at Sohmi's empty seat weren't enough, I even see Cherise in the hallway. It's no surprise that she turns and walks in the opposite direction.

I walk into the bio lab and see Garth lifting a microscope out of its case. Someone in an earlier class had pushed my stool to the other side of the room, so I drag it from the window and sit down next to him. It takes him all of thirty seconds to get the microscope and slide specimen set up. Most of the class is still struggling with how to open the microscope case, but Garth has no problem with it. He's so smart, and he knows everything. He reads almost as many books as I do, and he answers questions in class all the time. It doesn't take long for me to convince myself that he'll be able to help me. I have nowhere else to turn anyway, so I might as well try.

"Garth?"

"Yeah."

"Can I ask you something?"

"Sure can." He's hard at work adjusting the magnification on the microscope to bring the amoebas on the slide into focus.

"Do you . . ." Please, God. Just do me this one favor and make him know. "Do you know what a blessing is?"

"A blessing?"

"Yeah."

"Yeah. Who doesn't?"

I perk up and smile. My prayers are about to be answered. "What is it!? Tell me!" My heart is racing. Finally, the mystery will be solved. Garth is looking at me weird because my hands are gripped tightly around his forearm.

"That's when like a priest or clergyman . . ."

I drown him out and feel worse than I did before I asked him.

"Are you sure that's right, Garth?"

"Yes, Teenie." He rolls his eyes, and rightfully so. I've had him check to see if the amoeba had a cell wall for about ten minutes. "The amoeba is not a plant, or cyanobacteria, and therefore will not have a cell wall."

"Okay. I just wanted to make sure."

"Can I move on to question two now?"

"Yeah, I guess." I'm really trying to get into this. I don't want to think about whatever's waiting for me at four o'clock. Garth is already starting on question 3 when I say, "Wait, wait. What was question two about? You're going too fast."

Garth picks his head up from the microscope and tilts it straight back, looking at the ceiling. He takes a deep breath before turning to me and saying, "You want to help?"

"Yeah." I slide over a little closer, thinking he'll let me look at the specimen.

I reach out for the microscope and he says, "Umm. The lens is dirty. Can you go in the supply cabinet and get one of the cloths to wipe it off?" He's pointing toward the other side of the classroom.

It takes me a few moments to find it, but when I return to the desk, he's busy packing up the microscope. "What're you doing, Garth?"

"Oh, I'm done."

"What? Why didn't you wait for me?"

"Don't worry, we got a hundred."

"But I wanted to see it."

"Oh, sorry. I needed to get it done because I have to go to the library now."

Garth is one of the few students who can leave class early—he has so much work the teachers let him go as long as he gets everything in their class done. "Alright then. I guess I'll see you later."

If I thought I was feeling queasy earlier, the end of ninth period brings on a whole new level of anxiety. Part of me wishes I still had time to feel bad about Cherise and Crystal, but the butterflies are doing a number on my guts. I have only one hour left before I meet Greg. I'm as excited as I am scared. Look how the guy had me after just one kiss.

I spend the hour between the end of school and my meeting with Greg in the pizzeria at the corner of Fulton and South Elliott. Even though the garlic knots look good as hell, I'm too nervous to eat anything. Besides that, I don't want my breath to be kicking if Greg kisses me. That's if he kisses me again, and I sure hope he does. Tony the pizza man sees me smiling to myself and looks at me a little longer than normal. It's not unusual for me to study in here. He has a daughter, so I'm sure he has an idea of what I'm smiling about.

I start outlining my essay for Mr. Speight's class. It's an easy A for me, on how the railroads revolutionized commerce in the late nineteenth century. I want to get this out of the way early so I can spend the rest of the weekend studying for the math test. I finish the outline and glance up at the clock: 3:45, almost time for me to meet Greg. I pack my books up and head back to Tech.

The walk back to school is one of the most nerve-racking experiences of my short life. I can think of a million and one reasons to turn around and go home. But my legs and my curiosity, an even stronger sensation than what led me up to the attic, have overtaken my fear. Anything with Greg Millons *has* to be worth trying.

I get to the boys' gym door and look for a good place to wait for Greg. My heart is beating so hard I can feel it in my ears. I want to look as comfortable as possible, but I can't figure out if I should be sitting or standing. First I try sitting on the steps, but then I remember that my pants are yellow. I jump up and sweep the gray dust off my butt. Thankfully it doesn't leave a mark. Okay, so sitting is out.

Next I try leaning against the wall next to the door with my arms folded over my chest. I bend my knee and put my foot on the wall. This feels like a good way to stand because I *know* I look hot. Still, it's probably better if I wait until he comes out before I stand like this. My leg is starting to hurt.

Standing this close to the door, I can hear voices coming from inside the gym. I feel myself starting to get nervous again. Maybe I should have gone to the bathroom to make sure I don't have boogers in my nose. Oh no! What if I *do* have boogers in my nose or cheese stuck between my teeth? I didn't even check to see how my hair looks. I'm sure the hole on the waistband is showing too.

There's no time to pull my jacket into place, because the voices on the other side of the gym door are getting louder. It sounds as if they're really close to the door! I'm not ready to see him, so I fly down the stairs. The gym door swings open and hits the wall, right where I was standing a few seconds ago. Thank God I didn't stay there—that would've hurt. I stop moving and crouch so they don't hear me running down the stairs. Greg is talking. I recognize his voice right away and catch him mid-sentence saying, ". . . go ahead without me. I'll catch up with y'all tomorrow."

"Come on, son. Whoppers at Burger King for a buck-fifty." I can't see them, but that must be one of Greg's teammates talking.

"Forget a Whopper, man. I've got a date with destiny."

Hearing Greg say that puts a huge smile on my face and makes butterflies whirl around in my tummy.

"Which one is it now, Millons? A blessing or a blasting?"

"The first one . . . for now."

I do get a little nervous when I hear someone else say, "Damn, man, you stay lining them up."

"You know how I do."

They all start laughing.

"Aight, son. Go handle yours. See you tomorrow morning. Freakin' practice."

"Well, that's what happens when you guys don't act serious."

I duck down a little lower as Greg's teammates file out of the building. Greg goes into the hallway mumbling, "Where is this chick?"

After listening for a few more seconds, I hustle downstairs to the girls' bathroom in the basement. The faucet of the sink in front of me has been running since I walked in here, but the water is ice-cold. A chill runs down my spine when I splash a little on my face. I was hoping it would make me feel better and relax a little, but all it did was make me think about stuff more! A blessing, a blasting, I don't know which is better, or worse, or what the hell either of them is. Maybe I should leave. If I walk out of the building, I won't have to be scared anymore. But this is Greg Millons. The cute boy has *never* liked me, *ever*! This is what I've waited my whole life for. How can I turn this opportunity down?

My legs are shaking so much that I need to grab the sides

of the sink to support myself. I look at my reflection in the mirror and really see how panicked I look.

"Calm down, Teenie. Calm down." The sound of my voice is actually kind of soothing. I stare at my reflection and my eyes move to my shoulders. I'm half expecting to see a little angel on one and a little devil on the other. In all honesty, I would welcome the help.

The more I think about things, I realize the best thing for me to do is to leave. If I see him online later, I can just tell him that I felt sick. Yeah, I could tell him that I had a stomach virus and bad diarrhea. Okay, that's too much information. I'll just tell him that I had a stomachache and needed to go home. If I reschedule with him, at least I will have time to ask one of my friends what a blessing is.

After I take a few more deep breaths, I feel comfortable with my decision and turn the faucet off—well, try to. The knob turns but the water keeps running. I walk back to the bottom of the stairwell and listen for voices. There's no one up there, so I walk up the stairs toward the exit. My hand never reaches the door. I smell him before I see him. Greg grabs my hip and whispers into my ear, "You going somewhere?"

chapter 17

"So if everything goes according to plan, you'll see me all over *SportsCenter* next year."

Greg has been doing most of the talking since we started walking up the stairs. I try to nod my head and follow the conversation. I can barely hear anything because my heart is just thumping away. We just passed the fifth floor and I haven't done much more than smile. Even though I'm still petrified, the longer I'm with him, the more comfortable I feel. He's been complimenting me since the first floor, nudging me playfully while we walk up the stairs. I giggle when he says my butt looks like "an upside-down McDonald's sign."

"Damn, girl. You had me walking all over the first floor looking for you. I thought you dissed me."

"No way. I had to go to the bathroom." We're walking past

the sixth floor and I feel a lot better. I love the way he smells. I wish Cherise could see me now. She couldn't pull Greg Millons on her best day. Who's deadweight now? I'm still not sure where he's taking me and I can't really think of a cool way to ask, so I say, "Where are we going?"

"We're almost there. Just a little further. I want us to have some privacy."

Further or farther, I'll go wherever he wants me to go. My mother would probably slap me if she knew what I was doing, even harder if she saw how big my smile was.

As soon as we start walking up the last set of stairs, I feel his mouth and tongue on the back of my neck. There's a heat exploding all over my body and I start breathing really heavily. My back is to him, and he can't see me trembling and see how wide my eyes are open. I'm not sure what to do with my hands, so I keep them pressed against my side.

He takes off my book bag first, then my jacket, and rests them on the banister. His hands are all over me, grabbing, scratching. It feels so good. I feel the nails of his thumbs sliding along my waistline. He holds my waist in his hands and moves his fingers under my shirt. I can feel his tongue on my back and I moan a little.

He laughs and says, "You like that, huh?" His hands are huge but soft, every spot he touches tingles. He sits down on the stairs, and when he turns me around, he licks my stomach, sending shivers up and down my body. I don't even see when he unbuckles his pants. He moves up a few steps so that my face is lined up with his lap. I can see his, his . . . thing. He's reaching into his boxers.

My eyes get really big, and he smiles, a smile of confidence, as if to say, "Yeah, I know." He mistakes my look of fear as a compliment and seems confused when I say, "What're you doing?"

"What you mean?" He half smirks. "You said you was gonna hit me off."

"What're you talking about? I never told you that I would—" OH MY GOD!!! A blessing, he's talking about me giving him . . . ! I reach for my jacket and put it on. As I turn to walk away, he grabs me and nearly yanks me off my feet. The same hands whose softness I noticed earlier have an uncomfortable grip on my arm. I try to pull away but I can't. He's too strong.

"Where you think you goin'?" He's scaring me with the way he's smiling at me. He pulls me close to him, hard, until my face is inches from his. "Now you said you was gonna do this and you gonna do it." He said that as if I have no choice.

"No, Greg. I don't want to."

"But you said you was gonna do it. I said what's up with a blessing, and you said you would do it."

"But I didn't know what it was."

"Whatever. Don't gimme that. That's what I can't stand about y'all girls. Y'all be wearing all these tight clothes, getting brothers all charged up, and then be frontin'. You ain't doing that to me."

He pulls my arm so that I'm forced to lean forward. He's going to make me do it, whether I want to or not. I look up at him, hoping that the fear in my eyes will convince him to change his mind. I can see that if I don't do it, he might hurt me. It seems like my fear makes him more excited, because his smile gets bigger the more scared I look.

I don't know what else to do, so I grab it and start moving my hand up and down, just like in those movies that Cherise made me watch at her mother's house. He starts groaning and closes his eyes. I guess I'm doing it right. I turn my head because I know I'll cry if I look at what I'm doing.

"Yeah, that feels good. Now kiss it."

His head is tilted back and his eyes are closed. I leap at the chance to get away. When I reach for my things to run, Greg grabs the tip of my hood and rips it. As he pulls me in, I spin toward him and kick him in his balls as hard as I can. He lets out a whimper and crumples up at the bottom of the stairwell.

I don't stop running until I get to the downtown 4 train platform. It's only when I sit down that I feel my lungs and legs burning. I'm crying hysterically, the hood of my top is ripped. I can't believe he was going to force me to do that. What kind of girl does he think I am? I have to take some responsibility for putting myself in that situation. I should've known better. Him being a senior and me a freshman, what else was I expecting?

Attention, passengers. Due to a police investigation at Franklin Avenue, there will be delays on all Brooklyn-bound 4 and 5 train service. We apologize for the inconvenience.

A puddle of tears forms at my feet after five straight minutes of crying. I'm hunched over and what's left of my hood is wrapped around my face. I just want to go home. I wish there was a way I could just close my eyes and teleport myself into bed. I feel like such an idiot for putting myself in that situation. What was I expecting, for us to jump rope and play patty-cake? What a moron I am. How could I be so naive? I agreed to do something that I had never heard of before, so I have to accept blame for that. But I said no. My mother told me no means no, no matter what. He shouldn't have made me do that.

I feel someone nudge my shoe. I don't look up right away, thinking it was accidental. When I get bumped a little harder, I look up and see Passion standing in front of me. Crystal is standing behind her, two other girls are standing at her side.

"What's wrong? Why are you crying?" Passion sits down next to me and leans close. "It's okay. Tell me what happened."

I don't know this girl from Eve. I take a deep breath and say, "I'll be okay," hoping that will be enough.

"Just tell me what happened. Trust me. It will be better for you in the end. Just be honest with me."

"What?" Her friends have me surrounded.

"Now tell me the truth. What were you doing with Greg in the staircase?" She's very calm, which makes her even scarier, considering what she asked me.

"What?"

"I said what were you doing with my man in the staircase today?"

"Your man?"

"Yes. My man. When I heard he kissed you, it bothered me but I let it go. I see how you little sluts throw yourselves at him, so he's going to slip up every now and again. But then I heard what you had planned for today." She's shaking her head. "You're a shysty little hooker, aren't you?" She waits a few seconds before saying, "Well, don't you have anything to say?"

Oh no. Greg had a girlfriend and lied about it. Can it get any worse? I don't even know what to say. What can I say? I look over at Crystal, and she won't even look me in the eye.

"Hold up. What you looking at her for? I'm the one talking to you, not her. Tell me. Why were you in the staircase with my man?"

"I'm sorry. I . . . I didn't know he was your—"

"Okay, stop right there. You're a damn liar. I can't stand liars. I know for a fact that Crystal told you he had a girl, so don't make me slice your pretty little face open." She shows me the box cutter that's in her purse. "I already told you. Be honest and it will be better for you in the end. Don't make me say that again." She closes her purse and resumes questioning me. "Now. Tell me exactly what happened."

The tears are really pouring down my face. How did I end up here? How the hell am I going to get out of this?

"Leave her alone!"

We all turn at the same time and see Garth. He's trying to look tough.

"You better get outta here before you get hurt."

Judging from the look of Passion, I think she is the type to back that statement up.

"I said leave her alone." Garth's voice cracks. He's shaking like a leaf.

Garth is bigger than Passion, but that doesn't stop her

from walking over to him and punching him in his eye. Garth hunches over, holding his eye, but he gathers himself and stands his ground. Passion seems confused by his bravery.

"Oh, so you wanna be Captain Save-a-Ho now, huh? I got something for you." She reaches into her purse and pulls out the box cutter.

She pushes the blade out and gets ready to slash him but stops when a train comes barreling into the station. The Long Island Rail Road crowd bursts out of the door and forces its way between us. She puts the blade back in her purse, and I stand up and grab Garth's arm, pulling him into the train. The doors close before she has a chance to react. She stands on the other side of the door, glaring at me as the train pulls away, mouthing, "You're dead."

Chapter 18

"**W**hy is God doing this to me? Why?" Garth sits with me at the train station near my house while I try to compose myself. I've been sobbing for about forty-five minutes, boogers and all. He keeps passing me scrunched-up napkins from his book bag.

"Shouldn't you be getting home?" My nose honks after I blow into the tissue. "It's getting kind of late." Garth lives in the Bronx, about a two-hour train ride from my house.

"It's alright. I usually go to the library on Fridays, so no worries."

"Oh, okay," I say, trying my best to smile. "I'm sorry about your eye."

"Ahh, no problem. I've been hit harder." His eye is a little swollen and red. He's been rubbing it since we got on the train. "I sure am glad that I was able to find you."

"What were you doing at school so late anyway?" I'd been wondering how he just happened to be there to save me.

"I was hanging out. You know, just chilling."

The look on my face shows him that I find that hard to believe.

"Okay. I was tutoring a couple of the football players and . . . I asked them if they knew what a, what a blessing was, so . . ."

"So you stayed at school because I didn't know what I was getting myself into."

"I looked all over for you, but I couldn't find you. So I gave up looking and decided to go home. That's when I saw those girls bothering you from across the platform."

The way he's looking at me, I can tell he wants to ask me if I went through with it, but he would never make me feel uncomfortable. I don't have the strength to tell him the whole story, so I give him the short version. He never lets go of my hand.

"I saw him when I left school. I was wondering why he was limping down the street like that. That must've been some kick, Teenie. That'll teach him."

I laugh, and then we both sit quiet for a minute. I never realized how easy it was to talk to him. "I feel like such a loser right now."

"You know, Teenie, my mother says that God will never give you more than you can handle, and that if you have faith the size of a mustard seed, you can move mountains."

I nod my head, because my mother says the same exact

thing—well, at least the first part anyway. That mustard seed thing is something new, and pretty cool. "I'll make sure to pray the next time that crazy girl comes looking for me."

"I promise I'll be there if she does." His weak smile shows that he's just as afraid as I am. We sit in silence for a little bit before he says, "So what're you going to do now?"

"I'm not sure."

"Are you going to tell?"

"I'm not sure. I don't really know what I should do. I'm such an idiot." A few tears start to leak out of my eyes. Garth looks at me with a long face.

"I'm out of napkins."

I laugh and wipe my eyes with the back of my hand. "Why are you so nice to me, Garth?"

"Teenie, you're my only real friend. My brothers, all they do is give me wedgies and call me Nerdimus Prime. The guys on the football team only talk to me because I can help them stay eligible to play. I mean, I hang out with some of the guys from the Robotics Club sometimes but they're kind of boring. You've always been nice to me, no matter what."

"You're like my guardian angel."

"Lucky for you I'm not the kind that sits on your shoulder."

We both laugh, and I glance at my watch. "I think you should be getting home."

"Okay. But at least let me walk you home."

"I'll be okay. It's only a few blocks from here." I hug him and kiss him on the cheek. His face lights up like a Christmas tree.

"I'll see you on Monday."

"Bye. Get home safe."

Wow, he really likes me. I can tell by the way he's skipping across the street to the other side of the subway station.

I walk around the corner to my house. My mother has Fridays off, so I'm standing at the door with my ear pressed against it trying to time when I should go in. With a ripped hood, I want to keep contact with people to a minimum. I can hear laughter coming from inside. It sounds like my mother has guests. More eyes mean that someone will probably notice my ripped jacket. I tuck the hood into the neckline. I push through the door and see two pairs of size 13 Timberlands dumped near the doormat. Great. Just when I thought things couldn't get any worse, the twins are home.

Chapter 19

"Niblet!" they shout in unison. Bakari and Solwazi jump off the couch and rush over to give me a hug. Niblet was a name they made up referring to my lack of development in the chest area. They used to tease me and say that I would never have to spend money on bras, telling me that I'm so flat and skinny that I could slide into one of the rubber bands that Daddy brings home from his office.

My brothers are taller than Beresford but I'm a little shrimp like my mother, so I am being crushed between their hugs like a teddy bear. Most people can't tell them apart because they look and act exactly the same, finishing each other's sentences and posing as each other when they date different girls. I told one girl who was seeing Solwazi that Bakari had a small scar on his lip (courtesy of Beresford's spife). After

Bakari tried to kiss her posing as Solwazi, she slapped the mess out of both of them.

"Oh man. Don't look like we can call her Niblet no more," Kari jokes.

"For real. Did you go and save up your allowance for implants?" Solwazi leans in close to ask me that one, makes me feel like such a little kid.

These snaps are new material but not above any level that they've always thrown at me. With everything that's happened to me today, I just can't handle the onslaught. I turn to get away from them and I trip while I'm running up the stairs. They're laughing at me, calling me spastic. I wish they would just go back to where they came from. I can't stand them. Even after I close my bedroom door, I can still hear them laughing at the bottom of the stairs. What I wouldn't give for a grenade right now.

"Martine! Go wash up and come downstairs and eat! We ain't waitin' for you no more!"

That's the third time I've heard Beresford yell up. I'm sprawled across the bed with my face down and my head under the pillow. I've been in this position since I got home, and I don't have any intention of moving. My stomach is killing me. Thanks to Garth, I know that my stomach has its own nervous system, and my emotions can really make my guts twist and turn.

I don't want to talk to anyone. Wazi and Kari can go jump in a volcano. I'm sick of them making fun of me. Then there's my dad telling me what a bad daughter I am because I didn't tell him about what Cherise was doing. I wish I'd never even heard of Greg Millons. Then I wouldn't have to worry about his psycho terminator girlfriend trying to carve her initials into my face. I just want to press rewind and do things over.

I don't get it. I never cause any trouble. Truthfully, I have got to be one of the most considerate people on the face of the earth. I clean up after myself, I don't talk back to my parents, I eat—no, I actually *like* to eat—my vegetables, I study hard, I don't curse, I treat people with respect, I even leave the toilet seat UP when my brothers are home!

My mother says that I should treat people the way I expect to be treated. *Do unto others as you would have them do unto you.* Maybe I should flip that one around, something like *Before others do unto you, do unto them.*

"Yo, Niblet!" I hear a banging at the door, and Bakari pushes in. I pull the pillow tighter to the sides of my head to keep the light out of my eyes. "Mommy and Daddy said we can't eat until you come, so bring your narrow butt downstairs."

"I'm not hungry."

"What?"

I lift the pillow from my face and say, "I'm not hungry!"

"Oh, aight. Good. More shrimp for me." He slams the door and thunders down the stairs, saying, "She ain't coming."

Friday is usually date night for my parents and I have to fend for myself when it comes to food. Since my brothers are home, my mother cooked. My parents will know something is wrong when I don't come running for her famous curry shrimp. One of them will be here soon, so I hurry into the bathroom and turn the shower on.

I stop undressing when I catch sight of myself in the mirror. My hair is a mess and my eyes are puffy and bloodshot from all the crying. My face feels like my leather jacket, and there's a deep groove on my right cheek from having it pressed against the edge of my bed. Before the mirror fogs up, I notice a scratch on the side of my neck where Greg grabbed my hood.

The sound of my mother getting close to the bathroom door breaks my train of thought. I can tell it's her even before she yells, "Martine!" from the sound of her house slippers dragging across the hallway floor.

"Yes, Mommy!" I have to raise my voice to get it above the sound of the water hitting the bottom of the tub.

"You not coming to eat? I made your favorite."

"I don't feel so well! I'm gonna take a shower and go to sleep!"

"You want me to make you some soup?"

"No, thank you! I'll be okay!"

The door handle starts jiggling, and I hear my mother say, "Martine, open the door."

"I'm okay, Mommy! It's just a little gas! I'll be fine!"

My mother is not going to give up that easy, so I'm not surprised to hear her say, "Martine, open this door right now."

"Just a minute!" In less than five seconds, I strip off the rest of my clothes, jump in the shower, turn the cold water on while I cover my mouth to keep from screaming because I get scalded by the hot water, push the showerhead toward the wall to let the water temperature drop, and reach from behind the curtain to open the door for my mother.

"What's wrong, baby?"

"I'm not feeling so good. My stomach hurts."

"I'm going to make some soup."

"That's okay. I don't—"

"I'm going to make you some soup and bring it upstairs for you. Make sure you finish it all."

"Yes, Mommy."

"And since you not feeling well, I don't want you on that computer or phone all night."

"Yes, Mommy." It's not like there's anyone I want to talk to anyway.

With the twins downstairs, I'll be able to stay in the shower as long as I want. My father will be too distracted grilling them about school to keep track of how long I'm in here. No matter how many times I wash myself off, I still feel dirty. I start to soap my body again, but just sag to the bottom of the tub crying.

Sitting under the water reminds me of playing in the fire hydrant with Cherise when we were younger. Instead of smiling at what should be a nice memory, I cry even harder. All the kids on Cherise's block were jumping around, wetting passing cars, and screaming their heads off like it was the happiest day of their lives. It looked like so much fun, but I was afraid to join in because I knew it was illegal to turn the hydrant on. I've always been afraid. Doing things the safe way is all I know. After pulling at my arm for like fifteen minutes, Cherise persuaded me to join her and the rest of the kids. I had such a good time that day. Thinking back makes me realize how much I miss her.

I feel lost without her. She's the only person I can really talk to about this stuff. If Cherise were around, there's no way Greg would have been able to dupe me like that. Now I guess I can understand where she was coming from when she said she was tired of carrying me. What am I good for? I want my mother to hold me, but I can't stop crying long enough to call her.

All in all, I spend about forty-five minutes getting pelted by the water. The tips of my fingers are all wrinkled up, so I finally find a reason to get up. I'm just so confused. I've gone from sadness to anger to regret and back to sadness again. Now I just feel numb, and very tired. I can't dry myself off fast enough as I'm thinking about how badly I want to sleep.

chapter 20

I wake up to laughter, and it takes me a few moments to realize that I am on the receiving end of yet another prank by the twins. This morning, they used one of their old tricks, tickling my nose with a feather. They filled my right hand with some mess so when I went to brush away the feather, I smeared the stuff in my right hand all over my face.

They're laughing hysterically like two hyenas, closing the door just as my shoe bangs against the wall where Kari's head was. It's my fault for leaving my bedroom door unlocked. I had gotten used to them not being around, relaxed, and paid for it with a face full of shaving gel. A half a year in college, and they still act like little kids.

I look over at the clock and realize that I have overslept. When the twins are around, I usually wake up before them to keep them from catching me with one of their pranks. It's almost noon by the time I get into the shower. I slip on a big hoodie to cover the scratch on my neck.

When I finally make it downstairs, my mother is putting away the dishes from what must have been brunch. It smells like I missed some good stuff, but I still don't have much of an appetite.

"Morning, or should I say afternoon, sleepyhead."

"Good afternoon, Mommy."

"You feeling better?"

"I'm okay, I guess."

My mother reaches out and touches my forehead and then the side of my neck to see if I have a temperature. She just missed touching the scratch.

"You don't feel warm. Did you eat something bad yesterday?"

"I'm not sure. I can't remember what I had for lunch."

"You probably just need purging."

If my mother can't figure out what's wrong with a quick exam, she says we "need purging." I'm in no mood to be sitting on the toilet all day. I'll pass on her homemade prune smoothie—Drano Juice, as Wazi named it.

"What you got planned today? You and Cher—?" She pauses mid-sentence, remembering Thursday's falling-out. I'm sure the look on my face tells her that Cherise and I haven't patched things up yet.

"I have some studying to do. YSSAP stuff."

"Come with me to Flatbush Avenue. An hour won't kill you."

"No, thank you. I have a paper due, and a math test on Monday. Plus I have to finish washing—" I look up at my mother and realize she wasn't making a request. She looks over at me until I say, "Okay, let me go and grab my coat."

The corner of Flatbush and Church avenues is like the center of the Caribbean universe in New York. If someone is from the West Indies and they live in Brooklyn, they've spent at least one day in their life out here. My mother has been bringing me here since I was really small, and she knows to park a few blocks away instead of trying to deal with the crazy traffic.

Before my father started getting promotions, my parents used to buy everything here, from fruit to clip-on ties for my brothers. My mother came down here so much she was on a first-name basis with cashiers in like fifteen different stores. They practically rolled out the red carpet for her whenever we walked into Bobby's Department Store.

It's been a while since we've been on Flatbush. Now my mother does most of her shopping at Target and the twenty-four-hour supermarket. Flatbush was always a little different for me because we would visit such a variety of stores. I have to admit that it doesn't feel as fun as it used to. That could probably be because of my mood, but it is beyond crowded out here. Some little kid bumps into me and knocks the grocery list out of my hand. He's so busy sending a text on his cell phone that he doesn't even notice. To think, this little shrimp, he can't be more than seven years old, and even *he* has a cell phone.

"Martine! Come on!" My mother is standing at the entrance of the fruit stand, hollering my name down the street.

"Yeah, Martine, you better hurry up."

I turn around and see some cross-eyed boy smiling at me. I roll my eyes, pick up the list, and storm away from him.

By the time I weave my way through the crowd and into the fruit store, my mother has two cases of water and a basket full of yams and plantains resting next to our shopping cart. She has a trick for every fruit and vegetable to figure out if it's ripe. I still don't understand how she knows which honeydew melon is the sweetest just by plucking it. The ones I pluck all sound the same to me, but they never pass my mother's inspection. With the plantains, I think she's looking for a certain number of black spots: not too ripe, but just right. The one thing I *can* do is pick good okra. If the top snaps, I put them in a bag because that means they're fresh. This afternoon, she's already working on them before I get over to her.

"What are you doing, Mommy? You always let me do that."

"You outside acting the fool. I don't have time to wait on you to do it. I have to go to work."

"Why so early?"

"Early? Remember what time you woke up this morning? Shoot, it's getting late," she says, glancing at her watch. "Listen, I have to run over to the fabric shop across the street." She hands me three twenty-dollar bills and the car keys and says, "Pay for this stuff and wait for me in the car."

"Okay." I watch my mother hustle out of the store. As I turn back, I realize that the checkout line has grown to about ten people. Great.

After picking up the basket of yams and plantains, the basket of melons and cantaloupes, and the basket of string beans, broccoli, okra, squash, and carrots, my arms are burning like mad. I'm hoping to catch a break when I say, "Is it okay if I leave the water down here?"

The little old Korean lady smiles at me, shakes her head, and pats the counter, signaling me to lift the cases of water from the floor so she can scan the bar code. If she wasn't so little and old, or so cute, I would have made her come over and pick them up. I guess I'm at an age where I'm too old to pretend I can't lift it up and too young to flirt with one of the men in the store to help me. Lord knows where flirting got me yesterday.

After I pay, I start lifting the stuff down off the counter, and that's when I realize that it's going to be a pain in the butt to get it all into the shopping cart. Packing is not my forte, plus it doesn't help that the guy standing behind me is yelling, "Hurry up! I ain't got all day."

"Please don't ever yell like that again until you use Listerine, sir." Oh my gosh. I can't believe I just said that. Judging by the look on the man's face, neither can he. At least he's not yelling anymore.

I'm having a hard time dealing with the cart, and that's even before I realize how heavy and hard it is to maneuver. I manage to get close to the door after a bit of a struggle. There is a jam-up by the front, with people sifting through the peaches and plums. I'm about to say excuse me when the man I just finished yelling at starts pushing his way past me. I'm already halfway out the door. Instead of waiting for me to get out, he decides to squeeze by on my right side. As he moves by, he bumps into the bucket of codfish soaking in salt water and it spills all over my pants leg and down into my shoe.

"You stupid mother—" I don't get to finish my sentence because the little Korean lady is yelling her head off. She wants me to pay for the fish. I scurry out of the store as fast as my squishy shoe will let me. I've got the cart moving top speed when I get to the corner where I have to turn. I take the turn too hard, and one of the back wheels pops off and rolls into the middle of the street.

So I have an overloaded cart with three wheels and the right side of my leg is soaked in salty fish water. If there's any way that I could ever feel more uncomfortable than I do right now, I never want to know about it. My mother is already waiting at the car for me with an annoyed look on her face. When she notices the wheel missing, she walks over to me and starts lifting bags from the cart to lighten the load.

"What happened, Martine?" She catches a whiff of my stinky pants leg and says, "Phew. Never mind. I don't even want to know."

I'm not allowed to get into the car until my mother wraps plastic bags around my shoe and the bottom of my pants.

"Good Lord, Martine. Why couldn't you fall into some lavender or something?" She's fanning her face.

"It wasn't my fault, Mommy. Some stupid man pushed me."

"I don't know about you sometimes, girl. For someone who likes clothes so much, you sure do a good job of messing them up."

I give my mother two thumbs down for her lame joke.

"And speaking of clothes . . ."

She lets it hang in the air, but I'm not about to pick up the conversation. After a few moments, she continues.

"So what's his name?"

"What's whose name?"

"The boy."

"What boy?"

"The boy whose attention you're trying to get."

I mumble, "There is no boy," but it's not very convincing.

"Whenever things that weren't important before all of a sudden become important, there's ALWAYS a boy involved."

I don't respond. I focus my eyes on the traffic outside my window.

When we get to a traffic light, my mother puts her hand on my shoulder, then my chin. She turns my face toward hers. She moves her hands along her body and says, "It's not about this, it's about this," tapping her finger on her temple.

As soon as we get back to the house, I race upstairs and straight into the shower. My mother wasn't too happy about me leaving the groceries in the kitchen. I was not about to stay in those nasty clothes for another second. She knocks on the bathroom door, which is locked because otherwise I would be setting myself up for another prank from the twins.

"Martine."

"Yes, Mommy?"

"Are you washing the white clothes today?"

"Yes, Mommy."

"Okay. Don't forget about your dad's socks."

"Yes, Mommy." My dad goes to sleep with his socks on but slides them off his feet and pushes them to the end of the bed during the night. If he were here, I'd have half a mind to tell him to bring them downstairs himself. Saturday is dominoes with his Caribbean friends, so he's probably in someone's basement slamming tiles on a table and listening to loud soca music.

"And don't put them stinking jeans in my washing machine. If you want to clean them, use the hose in the backyard."

"Yes, Mommy." I already beat her to that one. I'll hide the sneakers and jeans in a garbage bag and throw them in the trash down the block when she leaves. I'm not even going to waste my time trying to clean them. It took me about twenty minutes to scrub the fish smell off my leg. I had to come out of the shower twice to find baking soda *and* vinegar.

When I'm done in here, I'm going to wash the last two loads, write my term paper for American studies, and study all day for my math test. I want to stay busy so I don't start feeling bad about myself, but there's no way I'm going to be able to get everything done. When my mother's dad died, she worked like a maniac. Beresford said that was how some people coped with trauma, like their brains just slip away. That's exactly how I'm going to approach this.

But of course, as with most plans, there are certain things that can't be accounted for. As I load the white clothes into the machine, I notice four gigantic laundry bags full of dirty clothes.

They look like the big piles of crap from one of those dinosaur movies, and probably smell just as bad. I guess the University of Maryland doesn't have washing machines. It seems like everything in the twins' closets is jammed into these bags.

After I turn the machine on, I go upstairs to finish putting the groceries away. I'm busy thinking about how little time I have when I hear my mother coming down the stairs saying, "Martine, do me a favor. When you finish with the groceries, clean the chicken breast for me and season it."

Great, more work for me to do. I'm about to ask her what happened to all of the shrimp when I look in the sink and see the Tupperware bowl that it was in completely empty. Solwazi and Bakari are so greedy. "Yes, Mommy." I wish she'd told me about the chicken before I packed it in the freezer. "Do you want me to cook it too?"

A really loud "NO!" comes from the living room.

My brothers may have had reason to avoid my cooking a few months ago, but I've been practicing, and my mother says I have the touch. Anyhow, now that I know the chicken is for their greedy butts, I might just season it with some Ajax.

"Thank you for helping me this morning, sweetheart."

"You're welcome."

"You feeling better?"

"I'm okay."

"Alright. Just relax today, but make sure you don't stay cooped up in your room."

"Okay." As long as she doesn't say I have to hang out with my evil brothers, I'm fine.

"Oh. And make sure you spend time with your brothers. You don't get to see them too often."

You gotta be kidding me.

Kari and Wazi are in the living room, watching basketball on ESPN. I slide onto the chaise and try to get into the game.

"So what's up, Nibs? How's your first year of high school going?"

I shrug my shoulders at Wazi's question and say, "Alright, I guess," before pulling my T-shirt over my knees. The house is kind of cool this afternoon.

"You doing alright with your tests and whatnot?"

I nod my head. If I have to sit here with them, I will make sure to keep the conversation to a minimum.

Kari is unusually quiet, curled up in the fetal position on the leather three-seater. His eyes are closed, and he looks like he's ready to roll right off the couch. I can't resist the temptation to ask him, "What's wrong?"

He starts groaning and writhing in pain. "I'm burning up. I feel like I gotta take a dump."

"So go do it then."

"I don't have to. It just feels like I do."

"Oh. Do you want me to make you some tea?"

"No. I just need some ginger ale." He groans and says, "I'm really starting to burn up."

"Well, since you're so hot, why don't you take off that sweater?"

"Just get the ginger ale please. I'm dying over here."

I look up at Wazi and hear him say, "This game is whack" as he starts flipping channels. I guess that means I have to get up.

As always, my mother is well prepared for the twins being home. The refrigerator is jam-packed with food, and I have to move stuff around. I didn't see any ginger ale when I put that stuff away earlier, and the fridge was basically bursting at the seams already. "I don't see it, Kari. You want some tea instead?"

"It's in there. I put it in there yesterday. It's on the bottom shelf behind the potato salad." He starts groaning louder and says, "Hurry."

I squat down to get a better look at the shelf. That seems like a dumb place to put the ginger ale. Then again, it's a typical move by one of the dim-witted Lashley men. I move the potato salad and see that there is something behind it. I grab the thing but the bottle feels kind of funny, like a ceramic pot or something. To get a better view, I bend down a little. When I realize what it is, I recoil with horror and let out a scream. They put Beresforda's ashes in the fridge. Who puts ashes in the refrigerator?!

When I turn to confront them, I see them both leaning into the kitchen from the living room.

"Why're you two always messing with me?!?!"

They are laughing as they run back toward the couches, Kari the loudest. Flames must be coming out of my nose and ears, because I can feel fire rising to my head. I'm biting down on my teeth so hard that I'm sure they're going to crack soon. I fling the refrigerator door open and grab the urn. I walk over to Bakari and dump the ashes onto his chest. He is so shocked that he doesn't have time to react and sits there as the gray cloud of dust spreads to his face. When I look over at Solwazi, I see that his eyes and mouth are wide open. For a quick moment, I think about smashing the urn over his head, but I flip it at him and storm up to my room.

The lights in my room are off as I sit on the floor with my back to my bed. My shirt is over my head, and my head is jammed between my knees. I've been rocking back and forth and gritting my teeth since I came up here. I just feel like screaming at the top of my lungs. I take my shirt off and flick it into the hamper. Normally I'm not an impulsive person, but it felt really good to just react for once. This feeling lasts all of five seconds.

What the heck did I just do? My father is going to kill me. Even worse, after that, my mother will revive me and kill me a second time. I just destroyed the only remains they have of their firstborn child. What kind of monster am I?

When I hear a knock at the door, I start crying. Oh God, enough with the crying already. I can't help it. It's like a monsoon of tears. I grab another T-shirt and put it on right before my brother pushes into the room.

"Niblet, you okay?"

"Leave me alone." I don't need to look up to know that it's Solwazi. He's always been a little nicer than Bakari, even though it was probably his idea to put Beresforda's ashes in the refrigerator. He usually ends up feeling bad when one of their pranks goes too far.

"Yo, we were just messing with you. I didn't think it was all that big, but you know, if it made you feel that bad, then that's not cool. So you know, I just wanted to come up and apologize."

He gets me a box of tissues and sits at the end of the bed. I wipe my face and blow my nose so hard that my ears get all stuffed up. When I look up, I see his lips moving but I can't hear a word he's saying. "What?" He repeats himself while I unclog my ears and catch him mid-sentence.

". . . to the park to play ball. You wanna come?"

"I'm not feeling so great."

"Oh, come on. We hardly get to play together. Me and Kari are going back to school on Sunday, so come hoop with us."

"What are you doing home anyway?"

"ACC tournament. The team is away, so we came home for the weekend."

"Redshirts don't travel with the team?"

"Budget cuts."

"Okay."

"So what's up? You gonna come play with us or what?"

"Go ahead without me. I really don't feel like playing. I have to study anyway."

"Come on, Nibs, don't be like that."

"Don't be like what? Every time y'all come up in here, y'all gotta be messing with me. I never did nothing to you."

Wazi stays quiet but never takes his eyes off me. He looks remorseful and I can tell that he is being genuine. "Okay. I understand what you're saying. But on the real, what you did downstairs . . ."

He's shaking his head. I knew I should've hit him with

that urn, should've just cracked him right upside his head. I don't want to hear nothing now.

"Martine, that was one of the funniest things I've ever seen." I wasn't expecting him to say that. "You should have seen Kari's face. He's gonna try and act like it didn't faze him, but trust me. He thinks you're crazy now, so you don't have to worry about him messing with you anymore. I know I'm not. I don't want no ashes or any other stuff thrown on me." He's laughing, and as much as I want to keep from smiling, one starts to crack through. I'm starting to feel a little bit better too.

My high-tops come flying toward the bed. One bounces off the mattress and lands in the trash and the other hits Wazi in the back of the head.

"Ay, yo! What're you doing, son?" Wazi's rubbing the back of his head, ready to throw my shoe back at Kari.

"Y'all coming or what? I got ankles to break and jump shots to make."

I guess I could play for a little while.

Chapter 21

"**Y**o, we got next."

There's only one court at Fortieth Park, so the other kids are all set to protest until they turn to see who called next. My brothers are basically legends here, and what they say goes. We used to come here every day during the spring when the twins picked me up from school. The basketball court is the only place where my brothers treat me with any kind of respect, even though they treat me more like a boy. I'll accept that. At least out here they don't view me as their object of amusement.

I go through my warm-up drills while they greet some of their friends from the neighborhood. Wazi and Kari were never skinny, but I am still surprised to see how much they've filled out. They're both wearing sleeveless tees, and the girls watching on the sidelines are getting all googly-eyed staring at their bulging biceps. And Kari has a tattoo! No wonder he was wearing that sweater in the house. He should know better than to have done that because Beresford will kill him if he sees it. Wazi sees me staring at Kari's tattoo, which looks like some kind of African symbol or something. He shrugs his shoulders while mouthing, "I told him not to do it."

I'm not the only girl that notices it. One of the little tramps on the sidelines is staring hard at Kari. He locks eyes with her, cracks a smile, and winks. He's so cheesy. His face looks a little duller than his arms, though. He still might have some leftover Beresforda on his cheeks.

We don't have to wait long for our turn to play. I'm trying to get focused, because when I play basketball with my brothers, I'm expected to play up to a certain level. Judging by the looks on the faces of the winning team, I know I have to bring my A game. As if their facial expressions weren't enough, one guy says, "Yo, what's going on here? Man, I ain't playing with no girls."

I haven't seen him in this park before, but I don't really come here without my brothers. He seems like a big talker, and I don't like him already.

"Don't sleep on her doggy," Wazi warns. "Don't say nothing when she hits y'all for like six, seven buckets."

"Yeah, whatever, man. I ain't playing with no girls. We won and we don't want no broads on the court."

"Yo, we got next. And she's playing," Kari says while stretching his quad.

The kid stares at my brother for a few seconds, then at me, before snickering and saying, "Aight. If y'all wanna play five against four. Check ball."

It's been a little while since I've played in a game, so it might take me some time to get comfortable. Luckily I'm matched up with a boy who's about my age, so I should be okay. There is something familiar about him. He doesn't act like he recognizes me, so I probably don't know him.

One of my laces is dragging on the ground and I bend down to tie my sneakers. The goofy kid with goggles that's on my team doesn't see me fixing my shoes and puts the ball in play. While I'm on one knee pulling my knot tight, the kid I'm supposed to be guarding cuts to the basket and puts in the first point of the game.

"Yo, hold up! She wasn't ready!" Kari yells.

"One–zip!" the talker barks, and backpedals down the court.

"Come on, Martine, let's go!" Wazi chastises me.

"Sorry. I didn't want to fall."

Wazi looks at me and shakes his head.

Kari inbounds the ball to Wazi, and he runs right through the defense to score an easy layup. The twins were always fast. They play a lot stronger than I remember, because Wazi took that ball to the rim with authority. The talker brings the ball back up and doesn't make one pass. He does a lot of fancy dribbling with Kari guarding him and pulls up for a long jump shot.

"Coming off," Wazi taunts as the talker misses badly. The

goofy kid on our team grabs the rebound and outlets the ball to Wazi. My brother takes off down the court and passes to Kari for another easy layup.

Before long, we're up seven to one. The twins are scoring with ease. I notice that every time they drive to the basket, my man starts to cheat off me to help on them. Kari drives and my man sags toward the basket, just as I thought he would. I slide down to the baseline and Kari passes the ball out to me. I let go of a jump shot and it goes right in, doesn't make a sound. Neither do the next seven jump shots I let go. The final score: Lashley Massive fifteen, Bum Juice Crew, as named by Wazi, three.

"That's game time, baby! And I told you, don't say nothing when she hits y'all for like seven buckets. My bad, I mean eight." Wazi and Kari start laughing and slapping each other five. The kids on the other team come over and say good game, but the talker storms off without saying a word.

"Now that's what I'm talking about. You're on fire right now." Wazi pushes my shoulder, acknowledging my great shooting.

After feeling crappy for so long, it's nice to crack a smile.

"Yo, go get the Powerade out of the car." Kari flips me the keys. My smile is gone. I hit eight jump shots and I'm back to gopher status already. I probably would have had to score every point for those duties to be taken away. When I get about fifty yards away, I hear Kari say, "Yo, Niblet!"

"What?!" I can't believe he's calling me that stupid name in public, God!

"Make sure the car ain't too close to the hydrant."

"What? Why?"

He points over toward the football field. There are about ten police cars double-parked on the street. I'm looking around to see if someone got shot until I notice a big banner hung up on one of the fences reading:

5TH ANNUAL NYPD VS. FDNY
FLAG FOOTBALL CHARITY GAME

I wonder why they picked this field to play the game. The field is all lumpy and the lines are faded. I know I've seen people walking their dogs and the folks in my neighborhood that walk dogs ain't too big on curbing them. At least the field looks better than the participants. New York's Finest, my butt. More like New York's Fattest.

I don't know why these big lummoxes want to embarrass themselves in front of all the little kids on the sidelines. Judging from their wheelchairs, I assume the kids are part of the charity this game is being played for. I guess no one told the snaggletooth woman in the crowd to watch her language. She's letting the referee have it, telling him things he can go do with his mother that might improve his eyesight.

"Niblet! Get the damn Powerade!"

"Alright, alright!!"

Looking through the cubbyholes and glove compartment of my brothers' Honda Accord reminds me how gross they are. There's an old apple tucked into the storage box between the two front seats and a rock-hard bagel half on the shelf of the passenger door. I turn my attention to the back of the car but it takes me a little while to find the drinks because Wazi stuffed them under the chair. Kari likes blue, Wazi prefers orange, and I'm usually stuck with whatever's left—in this case, red. I grab the three drinks and hit the door-close button on the remote.

There is another team ready to come onto the court, so I start to walk a little faster. From this distance, I see my brothers talking to a tall guy at mid-court. He has on a really nice light blue tracksuit with a matching hat and some white sneakers. My mouth is really dry. I decide to sneak a quick drink. I tuck Wazi's drink into the waistband of my shorts and put Kari's under my arm so I can open my bottle.

My drink never reaches my mouth. It falls right out of my hand and spills all over the ground. I turn around and start walking back to the car.

"Yo, bring the Powerade!" Kari shouts.

I don't want to go over there. My arms are shaking and I feel like I'm about to cry. I'm not going over there. I am going to stay here and deal with this bottle that I dropped. When I get to the garbage can, I realize that they are coming toward me.

Kari snatches his drink from under my arm and says, "Yo, Greg, this is my little sister, Martine. She's a freshman at Tech."

"What's up, Martine?"

My head is turned and my eyes are on the football field, so I don't know if he showed any sign of fear when Kari told him I was their sister.

"Ay, yo, just do us a solid and keep an eye out for her at

school." Wazi taps my shoulder to get me to take his drink out of my waistband.

"No problem, man. I'll definitely keep my eye on her."

"Appreciate it," Wazi answers, not even realizing the hidden meaning in Greg's comment.

"I heard she was out here torching my little brother just now."

"Oh, that was your brother? Son, she was giving him buckets from the corner." Wazi snickers a little after making fun of Greg's brother.

"Yeah, well, he's young and her jump shot is cash money. At least that's what I heard."

"Yeah, man. We've been training her since she was young." Kari turns to the court and yells, "Who's on next? Come on, let's go, let's go." He says, "Think fast" as he flips his Powerade bottle to me, then jogs back to the basket to get ready for the next game.

Wazi shoves the empty drink bottle into my hand and asks Greg, "How come you not playing?"

"Not today, man. I can't get hurt. I got a full ride to Duke, and the coaches told me not to play pickup games. Plus I got a play-off game on Monday. We just finished practicing."

"Duke? Alright. We're gonna be seeing plenty of each other next year then."

"Oh, that's right. Y'all are at Maryland. I gotta make sure I'm ready for y'all then."

"You gonna stick around for a little while, right?"

"Yeah, I just want to watch my brother play this last game, then we gotta flash."

"Alright, cool. Let's start this game up, then we'll talk afterward."

"Alright, fam."

Greg walks over to the bench.

"Nibs, let's go. Let's bust these cats and get out of here."

"I don't wanna play anymore. I don't feel well."

"Come on now. We only played one game."

"Can you take me home, please? I have a lot of work to do."

"Finish this game and then we'll leave."

They're not going to let me sit this game out, especially not after how well I played the game before. And come to think of it, if I don't play, I'll probably have to sit next to Greg on the sidelines.

The boy that was guarding me last game is back on the court. He's a miniature version of Greg. It's no wonder he looked so familiar to me.

"Yo, Collin, come here."

Greg's brother runs over to the sideline. Greg is giving him a pep talk and they both look at me and laugh. Before the game starts, Collin leans in close and whispers, "My brother says you can shoot because you have really soft hands."

The game is over before they even put the ball in play. Collin is running circles around me. I have no desire to play. Every time my brothers pass me the ball, my eyes are on Greg. When he sees me looking at him, he winks or blows a little kiss. It makes me feel worse and worse, but I can't stop looking at him. I've had a few passes bounce right off my body and straight out of bounds. When I do catch the ball, the results are no better.

"Martine, come on!"

Kari is frustrated when my last jump shot hits the side of the backboard. After that, they stop passing me the ball, and Collin starts clogging up the middle of the lane when my brothers take the ball to the basket. Since I am shooting so badly, I am a liability on the court and there is no need for him to guard me. The game is close even though I am a nonfactor. It ends as Collin scores yet another layup.

Kari slams the ball in frustration. "How'd we lose to them bums?"

Wazi turns to me and says, "Yo, what happened to you out there? How you go from can't-miss to can't-make?"

There's no need for me to respond to them because it won't matter what I say. They don't like to lose and get even more upset when the loss has nothing to do with how they played. At least I get the consolation prize. With the game over, I can finally go home and get away from Greg.

To be totally honest, it doesn't really bother me all that much that they're mad. Unfortunately, I am being subjected to even crueler punishment. The worst part is that Wazi and Kari have no idea what they're putting me through. They've been standing in front of me talking to Greg for the past fifteen minutes and I've had to sit here on the bench, waiting for them to finish.

"Me and Kari got red-shirted for this season, but we've

learned so much just from practice. I can't wait until next year so we can get some playing time."

"For real? Coach said as long as I show up in shape, I should get some burn next year."

"Yo, Greg, where you get them Jordans from? I haven't seen them in the store."

"I got a hookup with somebody at Nike."

"Them joints are hot."

"Thanks, man. You know I gotta stay dipped out for the ladies."

They all laugh, and I don't know what possesses me to look at them, but when I do, Greg is looking right at me, then looks away smiling. For half a second, I am so tempted to tell my brothers what he did to me and watch them stomp a mud hole in his butt. Then I remember all those cops on the football field and think better of it. As much as I would like to see Greg catch the beatdown of his life, I know my brothers wouldn't know when to stop. They would probably kill him based on what they did to a boy that pushed me off a swing when I was five. Then my parents would have to go and bail them out of jail, probably have to hire some big attorney to keep them from getting the electric chair or lethal injection. Wazi and Kari would have to explain why they beat Greg to death and it would all lead back to me, Martine the Mega-ho who goes into the staircase with boys.

Chapter 22

"**Y**o, son, did you see those Jordans Greg had?"

"And that chain around his neck was bananas."

"How 'bout that Lexus GS he pulled up in?"

"Those rims were official."

"Yes, sir. Where you think he's getting all that paper to buy stuff like that?"

"He's always been a shady dude. I wouldn't be surprised if he got some scam going on."

"Yeah, 'cause I'm saying, don't he live in the projects?"

"Exactly. SHAY-DEE."

"Well, whatever. That chain was still crazy."

"For real."

It's been Greg, Greg, Greg nonstop since we've gotten into the car. The twins have been talking about his clothes, his car, his little brother's clothes, basically comparing notes with each other on all of the flashy things he has. We're almost home, so I don't have to listen to this crap for much longer.

"Yo, bricklayer. Why you so quiet?" Wazi asks, looking at me in the rearview mirror while he swerves through traffic.

Just hurry up and drive and leave me alone.

"Yo, Niblet, you don't hear your brother talking to you?"

"Leave me alone, please."

"Leave you alone?"

"Yes. I'm not in a good mood, and you're starting to get on my nerves."

"What?" Kari turns around in the front seat to face me. "Get on your nerves? Nobody can't say nothing to you now?"

"Please, Kari. I don't feel like arguing. Just leave me alone." My voice cracks a little.

Bari frowns and fakes crying. "Boo-hoo. Look at you. Don't get mad at us 'cause you were playing like crap. Could've built a homeless shelter with all them bricks you were throwing up."

"Looking like Starks in game seven," Kari adds.

If my father didn't constantly talk about New York Knicks guard John Starks going two for eighteen in game 7 of the '94 NBA finals, I would have no idea what they were talking about.

"Well, you can't really blame her, son. We both know why she started missing like that."

"Yup. Cupid shot her right in her butt. As soon as she saw Gregory Millons, she was done. She couldn't stop looking at him."

"Yes, sir. She turned into mush."

192

"Can you PLEASE leave me alone?"

"Stop acting like a little girl."

"I am a little girl, yah jackass!"

"Who the hell you think you talking to?"

I turn back to the window and continue frowning, waiting for them to get to the house. God, please let me out of this car before I gnaw my brother's earlobe off.

Kari looks over at Wazi and says, "Jackass? You hear this, son? She's really bugging right now. You better check yourself, Niblet, before I tell Daddy that you dumped Beresforda's ashes on me today. No regard for your sister's remains. What kind of person are you?"

"You better check *yourself*, Bakari, before I tell Daddy about your tattoo. You know he would chop off your arm if he saw it. That's why you had it covered up today."

"Yeah, whatever."

Wazi snickers a little under his breath.

I'm on a roll, so I don't stop. "And don't even start with me or I'll tell Mommy that you had that ugly girl up in the house when they were on vacation last year."

Kari turns around and looks at me, shocked at first, then angry. He probably thought I had been sleeping when he brought that troll into the house, but I heard him telling her to be quiet even though he was the one making all the noise. "I don't know what you talking about."

"You know *exactly* what I'm talking about. Lynndonna Monroe, that ugly, cross-eyed Jamaican girl with the two-dollar weave who lives down the block." Wazi starts laughing loudly. "Yeah, and I don't know what you laughing about, Solwazi. I know you snuck her in the house a couple of times too."

"Yo, you ain't tell me that, son," Kari says to Wazi before throwing a mean look at me. "Whatever. Let's just leave Ms. Stankdraws alone."

"Looks like that arrow Cupid shot went right up her butt."

"I know, right? Acting mad stink since we've been home." Kari glares at me for a few more seconds, then turns around in his seat. "In high school now and don't know how to act." He shakes his head and starts changing the stations on the radio, then turning the volume up when he finds a song he likes.

When we pull up to the light, Kari turns to Wazi and says, "Ain't that that shorty E-ZPass walking into the Laundromat?"

"Oh yeah, that freak we used to . . .." He switches to the G-rated description when he remembers that I'm in the car. "Yeah, that girl that went to Tech. Damn, she's looking real nice."

Tech? By the time I look to see who they're talking about, the girl is already inside.

"Who's that thick chick with her?"

"I don't know. Let's go ask her."

Kari turns back to me and says, "We'll be right back, Miss Stinky."

"Where are you going? Please take me home now."

"That's the bus stop across the street if you're in such a hurry," Wazi laughs.

They shut the car off and walk into the Laundromat. It doesn't matter that I want to go home. When they see girls, the little brain function they do have shuts down. Their hormones take over. I don't feel like waiting anymore, and if they had left the keys in the ignition, I would have tried driving home myself. We're only about six or seven blocks from the house. When they disappear into the Laundromat, I get out of the car and start walking.

I can cut through the alleyway on the next block and shave about three minutes off the walk. All I can think about is jumping in my bed, sweaty clothes and all. Then again, I might want to take these clothes off, because the wind just blew and I feel a shiver run down my back. I hear someone honk from a passing car and say, "What you doing out here all by yourself?"

Shame and disgust overwhelm me when I realize who it is. I start walking faster when I hear the door open, unsure if I should break into a full sprint. By the time I think about running, Greg has grabbed my arm.

"Hold up, hold up."

"Leave me alone," I say, snatching my arm away.

"Oh, come on. Don't be like that. I just wanna talk to you real quick."

"What's there to talk about?" I cross my arms and put my meanest face on. It's a total front, because I am scared out of my mind.

"Things didn't go exactly the way we planned yesterday, did they?"

I shake my head and look away, but my arms stay crossed.

"Did you tell anyone what happened?"

"Why?"

"It's probably better if we keep things between us until we get a chance to do it the right way."

I turn to walk away but he grabs my arm again, not as gently as the first time. "Where you going? Mmm. You're still sweaty." He licks the hand that he grabbed me with. "Now we definitely gotta do it right." The way he said that, I can tell he's grinning. I'm trying my best not to look at him.

"Let go of me, please."

"When we finish talking. So you didn't tell nobody, right?"

"Just let me go."

"I *said* I'll let you go when we finish talking. How long are your brothers in town for?"

"Why don't you ask them yourself?"

He turns his head fast, I guess to see if they're coming. "Smart move not saying anything to them. Those are my boys and they ain't gonna believe you anyway. Nobody's gonna believe you. Plus, if you really wanna go to Spain, it might be in your best interest to keep our little thing a secret. You know what I'm saying?" He starts rubbing my arm and then says, "So Monday, after school. We'll finish what we started, right?"

I don't answer him. My heart is racing and I don't have the courage to say anything else.

"You want a ride home?"

I keep quiet.

"Alright then. I'll see you at school." He leans in and kisses my cheek.

When Greg drives away, I slump down onto the steps of the house I'm standing in front of. My legs feel like noodles and start shaking once I take my weight off them. Why didn't I run? Or scream? Or kick him in the nuts again? Why did I let him rough me up like that? He's cute and he's so popular and all the girls want him. Maybe I wanted it just like they do. I did want it. Who am I kidding? I knew what was going on, and I should've known better.

A car pulls up in front of me. I guess Greg has come back to do what he wants with me. The horn honks, but my head stays down until I hear my name called.

"Niblet. Get in the car."

The horn honks again, and then I hear the door open and slam.

"Martine. Get in the car."

I look up at Kari, but I don't move.

"Yo, what's wrong with you? Get in the damn car."

He grabs my elbow, drags me toward the car, and sits me down in the backseat. Wazi pulls off as soon as Kari closes the door. Kari swivels around in the passenger seat to face me and I can see Wazi looking at me in the mirror.

"Yo, why did you get out the car like that? You know Daddy would have a fit if we went home and didn't know where you were."

"Niblet, what's going on with you?"

"I'm fine." Just fine.

Chapter 23

There's no more denying it. I officially miss my best friend. There's not a thing I wouldn't give to be able to talk to her and figure out what the hell I'm supposed to do right now. Even though I still think she's a major B for treating me the way she did, part of me is worried that she might still be seeing that stalker Big Daddy.

I know I'm desperate, but it's not like I have much to choose from. Of my friends, Garth is by far the easiest to talk to because he's such a great listener, but what kind of advice could he give me? The guy fainted during health class last semester when the teacher said the word "testicles." There's no way in hell I'd tell my brothers. I don't feel comfortable talking to any of the girls from the lunchroom. Sabrina would find a way to make me feel bad with one of her offhand comments, Sohmi would just look at me with her mouth wide open, and if I tell Malika, I'd basically be telling two people, because as sure as the sun comes up she would end up telling Tamara.

That leaves my mother. She told me that I could talk to her about anything, and she's been telling me that since, since . . . well, ever since. No matter the subject, she told me that I could come and talk to her whenever I had an issue.

We have to get up early for church tomorrow, so I don't have much time to sit with her. She got home at around eleven, and I know she has to catch up on some sleep. The door of my parents' bedroom is closed. I raise my hand to knock on the door, but I hear noises coming from downstairs. I peek down the staircase and see them snuggling on the couch, watching some loud movie on HBO. As I walk down the stairs, I start to lighten my footsteps when I realize Beresford is talking about Cherise and her mother.

"That woman still ain't call me yet to find out about she daughter. I tell you, these people don't watch what their children doing and all manner of craziness does go on."

"Did you try to call her?"

"Me call she? Come on, Glory. If somebody did leave me a note concerning my daughter, you think they would have to contact me again?"

"That's true. Well, maybe Cherise never left the letter in the first place."

"That could be true, you know. I tell you, that girl fast, and she mother ain't no better. Running all over the place with them young fellas."

"She's not even thirty yet, Beres. She had Cherise when she was fifteen. But I agree with you. She should be more involved in what her daughter is doing, because if someone tried to take advantage of Martine like that . . ."

"One of us would be in jail for sure, 'cause that man woulda get chop up. But that little girl should know better than to be putting sheself in situations like that. Thank God Martine don't get on like that. I tell you something, though. I worry sometimes about Martine hanging around Cherise."

"You place too much weight on Cherise's influence and not enough on your daughter's common sense. They've been friends for ten years and we haven't had a major problem yet."

"You're right. We're lucky we don't have to deal with her doing foolishness and crap."

"Martine? You need something?"

Oh, shoot! How did my mother know I was here? "Yes, Mommy. I just wanted to talk to you for a minute."

"Come."

I continue down the stairs and see both of them smiling at me. My parents think so much of me. How would they feel if I told them about what I did after school yesterday? Or about what happened to me today?

"What is it, dear?"

I am trying to think of a nice way to tell Beresford that I want to talk to Mommy alone, but as usual, my mother reads the situation. "Beres, I bought some cookies-and-cream. Can you please make me one of your famous sundaes?"

"You did buy ice cream? I didn't see it in there!" My dad

jumps up off the couch and runs straight for the freezer like the ice cream is trying to escape or something. He'll be in there for a few minutes, so my mother and I will have some time alone.

"I don't want you to be disappointed with me, Mommy."

"I will try my best, darling."

"Mommy." She's smiling at me and stroking my hair out of my face. I can't do it, not after listening to my parents talk about what a good kid I am. I can't tell her, I just can't. "I don't think I'm going to be able to handle all the laundry. I didn't expect the twins to bring home so much stuff. I'm not going to have time to study."

"I figured that. No problem. Well then, you know what you gotta do."

"Yes, Mommy."

"I want to be clear. It's a ninety-five average that you're going to get, right?"

"Yes, Mommy."

"Okay. I spoke with your father, and he agreed to let you go. BUT . . . you have to make sure that you stay out of trouble in the interim. I don't want to see any of this mischievous behavior, young lady. Keep your nose clean."

"Yes, Mommy."

"Glory, you want sprinkles on it?"

"Yes, Beres," she calls back before returning her attention to me. "Is there anything else?"

"Martine, you want one too?"

"Okay, Daddy. But a small one."

"Is there anything else, sweetheart?" my mother asks again.

"No, Mommy."

"Okay then. Guess you better go upstairs and hit the books. You have a lot of work to do."

"Yes, Mommy."

I wish I could say I feel happy at not having to wash my brothers' clothes. I have to study twice as hard to raise my average two points. With all this crazy stuff going on, how in the world am I going to manage everything? I'm willing to bet something else will go wrong now. I'll just sit here and wait for the phone to ring telling me that my grandmother is dead. Or better still, go digging through my parents' stuff and find out that I'm adopted. Who cares anyway? Not like I could feel any worse.

What sucks the most is that I'm working on what should be the easy stuff, my paper for American studies. The only thing I'm able to concentrate on is the blinking cursor in my Word document. At this rate I'm going to be up all damn night. I can already feel my eyes starting to burn. Maybe if I grab some caffeine, I might be able to get this stuff done. For there to be any hope at all, I have to finish this paper tonight.

I open my bedroom door and hear the TV still on. When I reach the bottom of the stairwell, I see my parents snuggled together asleep on the couch. I put a sheet over them and smile. They actually look kind of cute up until my dad stirs and busts a big old fart. Nice.

Chapter 24

All I want to do is sleep—lie down in my bed and never wake up. I hardly got any work done last night. Every time I started writing a sentence for my paper, I kept thinking about what Greg did to me. It was pointless to keep trying. Before I slunk into bed, I took a couple of dark sheets and hung them over the blinds. I didn't want any light to seep in and disturb me.

My eyes pop open and I stare at the alarm clock until the numbers come into focus. No matter how hard I try to go back to sleep, I can't relax. Any minute now my mother will push into my room and wake me for church. If I had it my way, I would stay in bed for the whole day.

My mother comes into the room singing a song by Luciano called "Lord Give Me Strength." It's a song that I hear maybe once every two months or so. When she does sing it, it's always on Sundays, but I've also heard her hum it under her breath when Beresford starts getting on her nerves.

She's halfway through the second verse, and I haven't moved a muscle. My eyes are slammed shut, and I do my best to pretend I'm still asleep. The release of the sickly groan I'm holding in has to be timed just right. I know it's perfect when I hear my mother say, "Oh, sweetie, you still not feeling well?"

I shake my head. There's genuine concern in her voice. This might just work. She puts her hand on my forehead and neck. I'm trying to will myself to feel hot, but when she shakes her head and says, "Okay, Martine. Up, up. In the shower," I am disappointed yet again.

"Wait, why in here so dark?" She flips the light switch on. I hear her gasp when she sees my clothes dumped at the foot of the bed and three empty cans of Coke on the nightstand. "Martine, what's going on here? Why does this room look so messy?" My mother snatches the sheets off the blinds and opens the windows. "In here smells closed up. When we get home from church, straighten up this room. I didn't raise you like this."

When she walks out, I get up and turn the lights off and go right back into the bed. I don't want to get up, I'm not going to get up, and I don't care who comes in here and tells me different.

About fifteen minutes later, Beresford knocks but doesn't wait for an answer. "Martine. Come on, sweetheart, get up. Time for church."

I close my eyes and pretend that I'm sleeping again.

"Martine. Get up. It's time for church."

I try to use the groan again and say, "Daddy, I don't feel well."

He doesn't have nearly the level of patience that my mother has, so I'm not surprised to hear him suck his teeth and say, "Girl, get up and go in the shower now. Sloth is a sin, yah know."

I try to stay quiet and hope that he'll disappear. It's a trick I've seen Wazi and Kari use. My father usually gives up trying to wake them after a couple of minutes.

"Martine! You ain't hear what I tell you? Get off yah tail and go in dee blasted shower now!"

He's going to stand at the door until I swing my legs out of the bed and I get into the shower. When I finally make my way out to the hallway, I peek into the twins' room and see Solwazi's crusty foot hanging off the edge of his bed.

"Why do I have to go if they don't have to?"

"Those heathens are in God's hands now. You're still in mine."

I knew he was going to say that.

"But wait. Martine, where all this back talk coming from?"

I close the bathroom door without responding.

"Come on, Martine, hurry up."

My parents are walking so fast that I can barely keep up with them. Because of my little mini-tantrum this morning, we're late to church. It usually takes about ten minutes to find a parking spot, so my dad likes to get here nice and early to beat the crowd. We end up having to park about four full blocks from the church, and Beresford is not happy about that at all. He's grumbling about missing the offering. I wish he took so much pride in giving me my allowance.

My father tried to explain tithing to me, but I don't think I'll ever understand why I have to give ten percent of my money to a church whose coffers are overflowing. With the way my parents give to the church, they probably paid for at least two of the Persian rugs hanging on the walls.

According to Beresford, this is where we belong. I was relieved he finally figured it out, because it took us a good six months to find the "right" church. My father's take for all the searching was "Why must I sit in a boring church and listen to a preacher that don't know he elbow from he backside?"

My mother was not happy about the size of the Christian Center of Worship and Praise, and seemed somewhat intimidated. The church she grew up in back in Grenada was much smaller and didn't have "all this pageantry and grandeur." She was resistant right up until she heard the dynamic preaching of the pastor, Dr. N. Nathaniel Bailey. I would never think to use the word "dynamic" to describe the pastor, but that's what it said on the back of her book. Oh, and my mother also loved that Pastor Bailey was a woman. I actually liked the church we went to before CCWP and hoped that we would have stayed there, but once I saw my mother's face, I knew there was no hope.

According to Pastor, Sunday is supposed to be a day of rejoicing, a day to feel great and go into the week feeling unstoppable. Not today. When the usher greets us at the door and asks me if I'm blessed and highly favored, I have to bite my tongue to keep from saying no. My dad starts to give me looks when I don't return the good-mornings of the other churchgoers. What's so good about this morning? What in life is good enough for me to smile and talk with someone who doesn't even know my name and would probably knock me over if I sat in their seat today?

My dad is fed up with my attitude. Before we walk to our seats, he pulls me aside. "Look, I don't know what is going on in that head of yours, but you better get yourself settled. This is a house of worship, and I will not tolerate you being rude and unmannerly. Is that understood, young lady?"

I roll my eyes at him and say, "Yes, Daddy." I just rolled my eyes at my father. I don't think he noticed, because he starts walking toward the door to the auditorium. It didn't escape my mother's attention, though. Just the look on her face makes me regret it immediately. "Sorry."

She shakes her head and walks after my father.

Normally we sit in the front of the balcony, but since I took my "sweet time" getting ready, we have to sit in the second-to-last row. Pastor Bailey comes out onto the stage and greets everyone. "Good morning, CCWP. How are you feeling today?"

"Blessed and highly favored," the congregation responds as one, pretty much everyone but me.

"Yes, we are, aren't we? Let us stand and pray."

I never pay attention during this prayer and usually spend the two or three minutes looking for the worst-dressed person in church. This morning, it's a toss-up. There's a man at the end of my row who's making my eyes hurt with his green and yellow pin-striped suit and shoes to match. His competition is a woman, shorter than me, with a giant black lampshade hat. Pastor Bailey finishes the prayer and says, "Now turn and give about three of your neighbors high fives and tell them 'God is awesome!'"

My hands are at my sides, and I'm staring into space so I don't have to look at anyone. I can feel both of my parents looking at me disapprovingly. When we're given permission to sit, a feeling of sleepiness takes over immediately. I am having trouble getting into the lesson, something about God changing Abram's name to Abraham. Pastor Bailey has called out a bunch of verses, but my Bible is on the floor between my feet. My dad taps my elbow when I start to nod off. Every time I try to concentrate, my eyes start to cross and my head drops. My little naps don't last long, because my dad keeps waking me up. I wish he would stop doing that. It's really annoying.

My mother passes me a Halls, and the menthol hits me right away. I roll my head around a few times and try to listen to Pastor Bailey.

"I remember one sister telling me that she was having problems with her husband. She said, 'Pastor, I can't take him no more. I'm going on vacation.' I know this sister very well. Whenever things aren't going right with her husband, she's on the first plane to Aruba. She's so busy running that she won't sit still and listen. God doesn't yell, He whispers."

I always expected God to have this booming voice that would shake a room. In reality, the few times in my life that I have prayed, the answers usually came to me during quiet time.

Pastor continues, "I told her, 'Sister, you can't run away from your problems. You'll run out of money first.'"

That draws laughs and applause from the congregation.

"Aruba is expensive," she says, chuckling a little.

When the laughter dies down, she continues, saying, "God doesn't give us more than we can handle, people. He is testing your faith. When things are going good, most of us don't give thanks for that."

That's true. I don't think I've ever prayed when things were going well, and judging from all the heads I see nodding in the congregation, a lot of people feel the same way.

"It's only when things get rough that we run to Him. Here is where the problem lies. We think we're in control of everything. When things don't go our way, we get upset and start questioning God. *Why is He doing this to me?* We need to change the way we think. Don't make idols of your circumstances."

I'm not sure what that means until she says, "Don't let your problems dominate your thoughts. Your mind should be on God and His bountiful grace."

Okay. I guess that makes sense—a little at least.

"He has a plan for us, and we don't have the ability to understand it. God has our lives on autopilot. If you apply enough force, you can turn your life in a direction that He did not lay out for you. Think about how much energy you have to apply to do things your way. We have to let go, people. We have to let go and let God."

A man in the crowd shouts, "Preach it, Sister," and the applause starts to get louder.

"If He brought you to it, He can get you through it! Take your hands off the wheel and let Him do what He does best!"

The church is on its feet, and everyone is clapping loudly. I stand up too and silently say to myself, *If He brought me to it, He will get me through it.*

I feel a little lighter after church. I don't understand why God is putting me through this, but the only way I'll be able to deal with what's happened is to be faithful. Even though I feel like a phony saying that, I'm really going to try to hold on to it.

After service, my parents stop at a diner for brunch. The diner is one of the few places where my mother will allow us to eat. Normally we talk about random things, but something is in the air today. I get the feeling that they are worried, so I'm not surprised when my mother says, "Martine, we're concerned."

I wait a few seconds and then ask, "About?"

"Well, sweetie, you've been acting a little strange lately."

I sit quiet and play with my pancakes.

"You haven't been eating. Are you sure you're okay?"

"I'm okay. I'm just a little tired."

"I know you're under a lot of pressure with this scholarship thing. Do you think maybe you should wait until next year?"

"No, I still want to do it. I don't want to wait."

"So what's wrong? Tell us what's bothering you."

"I'm fine. I'm just tired. That's it."

As usual, my mother is going to press until she gets an answer that she's satisfied with. "Are you still upset about what happened with you and Cherise?"

"Yeah. A little, I guess."

She reaches out and grabs my hand. "Martine, I want you

to understand that these things happen all the time. I could tell you dozens of stories about how I lost friends and felt horrible about it afterward. I just want you to remember that we are always here for you, no matter what."

I nod my head and keep my eyes fixed on the piece of pancake I've cut. I've been trying to get every part of it covered in syrup.

"When something is bothering you, we want you to talk to us about it, okay?"

"Yes, Mommy."

My mother reaches for her cell phone.

"Yes, Bakari. We're at the diner." She stops and listens, while my dad signals for the waiter to come over. "That is what both of y'all want? Cool yah nerves, boy. You talking too fast. Which one have the turkey bacon in it? Okay."

The waiter comes over, and my dad says, "Boss, I need to make an order for takeout. What they want, Glory?"

"Okay. We'll be home in a minute." My mother closes the cell and says, "Two fried eggs with turkey sausage and two scrambled eggs with cheese and turkey bacon. Both of them with home fries."

If it were up to me, I wouldn't get those two mongrels anything. Sunday brunch should be reserved for people who go to church. My mother turns to my dad and says, "I tell you, those boys are your children," as if my father doesn't already know that those two Decepticons are a chip off the old block. He nods his head, probably not even hearing a word she's saying because he's too busy staring at soccer on the TV. My mother looks at him and shakes her head.

When my brothers go back to school, I finally get a chance to sit down and tackle my studying. I finish my American studies essay, but I need Garth's help for this math test because it will be, by far, the biggest challenge for me.

```
Appletini: explain it to me one more
    time?
Garth Vader: Ok no problem.
```

I need at least a ninety-four on this test to get that scholarship, and that's only if I get hundreds on my American studies essay and the English test I took last week. All my other grades are pretty much set. They're all worth twenty percent of my grade for the semester, so I have to make sure I do well on all of them. This is going to be really hard.

```
Garth Vader: when you have a fraction
    in front of the variable, the easiest
    way to figure out the value of the
    variable is to multiply the entire
    equation by the inverse of the
    fraction.
Appletini: huh?
```

Looks like we're going to be here all night. I hear Beresford and his lead feet coming up the stairs. He stops at my door and pokes his head in.

"Ayy."

"Hi, Daddy."

"What you doing?"

"Studying for an exam tomorrow." My eyes don't move from the screen.

When he sees my Instant Messenger flashing, he asks, "Who you talking to?"

"One of my classmates from school."

"It's a boy?"

"Yes."

"Who?"

"Garth."

"Who's Garth?"

"One of my classmates from school."

"How old he is?"

"Fourteen. He's helping me study for my math test."

"Okay." My dad looks at the screen, probably trying to catch a glance of what I'm chatting about. "Alright. Remember to be mindful of what you're doing on that computer. I ain't want you on there all night, yah hear?"

"Okay, Daddy." Thanks, Cherise. Whenever my dad thinks I'm talking to a boy, he's going to grill me like a piece of chicken.

He sticks his head back into the room and says, "Martine, I want you to know that if there is something bothering you, you can talk to your mother and I about it. We love you very much and don't want you to feel like you can't come to us if you're having a problem or you find yourself in a situation that is above your head."

"Okay, Daddy. Thank you."

"Good, good." He taps the wall and walks out of the room.

Garth is really being patient with me. We're working on twenty questions that he put together from Mr. Gershik's old exams.

> Garth Vader: the key is to study smart
>   Teenie.
> Garth Vader: I've looked at his tests
>   from the last 5 years and it looks
>   like he uses similar questions on all
>   of them.

With the way things have been going for me, I'm all but assured that he'll use new ones. Not like it would matter anyway. If we're studying smart, I must be a giant idiot, because we've been stuck on this same question for thirty minutes. I haven't even told Garth what Greg said to me. What's the point of me studying like this if he's just gonna take it away from me?

> Appletini: I give up Garth. I can't
>   get this. It's too hard.
> Garth Vader: no you're not and yes you
>   can. Let's try it one more time
> Appletini: I can't do it!
> Appletini: it's too hard. I can't
>   concentrate.
> Garth Vader: relax and take a deep
>   breath

Appletini: but I don't know the
    answers to any of these problems.
Garth Vader: we have to focus on one
    at a time.
Garth Vader: deal with this one first
    then move on to the next otherwise
    you get overwhelmed by everything.
Appletini: words of wisdom from your
    mother I suppose?
Garth Vader: lol. yup. If it wasn't
    for her encouraging me, I would have
    crumpled like a cheap suit.
Garth Vader: focus on one thing at a
    time.
Appletini: alright

Ten more minutes and I feel like I'm going to smash my
keyboard, but Garth is still here, holding my hand.

Garth Vader: therefore, once you turn
    the coefficient into a whole number,
    x has to equal . . .

I've done the calculations four times, and I keep coming
up with the same number.

Appletini: 11?
Garth Vader: correct!

Chapter 25

In the morning, my mother sings "Three Little Birds," her usual song. I will do my best not to "worry about a thing," and try in my heart to believe that "every little thing is gonna be alright." The lesson at church helped a little, but in all honesty, it's kind of hard to be strong when I know there are people in school ready to bash my brains in.

Beresford almost breaks the bathroom door down because of how long a shower I take. He's so angry when I come out that he can't even form a proper sentence, although I do hear a few high-pitched noises and something about him cutting off the pipe. When I get out of the shower, I switch outfits about ten times, trying anything to prolong having to go to school. I thought about pretending to be sick—but after Sunday and the look on Beresford's face this morning, I don't want to press my luck.

I try to take my mind off things by rereading my essay for Mr. Speight's class during the train ride. The essay is really good and I'm satisfied that it's A+ material, but I still can't shake the unease. I've been singing "Lord Give Me Strength" to myself all morning but there's a pit in my tummy the size of a basketball. I don't even know why I'm reading this stupid paper anyway. It's not like I can make any changes at this point. The math test is more pressing, because I'm not as confident that I can get the grade I need.

My mother is a firm believer in how negative thinking can lead to negative outcomes. It appears that she is right and that I've sealed my fate by thinking about how bad things are for me. When I get out of the train and start walking down the platform, I see Passion and her crew waiting by the turnstiles across the tracks. With the way she is scanning the faces in the crowd, I can tell that she is waiting for me, waiting to finish what she started on Friday.

She looks especially mean today with her cornrows and Timberlands, a hairstyle and shoe that I've seen many girls wear when they're ready to brawl. Cherise told me that girls put a ton of Vaseline on their faces to keep from getting scratched. The reason for the Timberlands is obvious: they're the best stomping shoes money can buy. I can see Passion's face shining from all the way over here, and her boots are laced right up to the top. It's a good thing that I know this train station like the back of my hand. There are at least five other exits I can use to avoid crossing paths with her. I take a detour that leads me farthest away from her and end up coming out of the station two blocks out of my way.

When I get into school, I don't feel any safer. If I only had to watch out for one person, I think I would be able to make it through the day. Having to stay away from two people will be damn near impossible, especially when one of them knows my class schedule. As soon as I turn the corner and see Greg leaning up against the wall of my class, I feel the air go out of my body. He hasn't spotted me yet, so I turn around to walk in the opposite direction. Unfortunately, my stealth act is short-lived, as I bump right into Cherise and knock her iPod out of her hand. Things get even worse when I hear Greg say, "There you are."

He puts his hands around my waist and jerks me around so I'm facing him. He pulls back on the side of my jacket and says, "Nice shirt."

Cherise walks by and sees the fear in my eyes. She pauses for a second before walking through the doorway to class. I don't care how mad I am at her. If I saw a guy roughing her up, I would help her.

Greg has a hard grip on my pelvis and a scary smile on his face. "So we're still on for this afternoon, right?"

I look down and say, "Leave me alone." He grabs my chin and forces my head up. His smile is gone. "Get off me!" I try to move my head away, but he holds it in place.

"We already talked about this!" He looks around to make sure that no one is paying attention to us, then guides me over to the wall with a tight grip on my arm. There are a few students walking by. Greg has me pinned against the wall in a way that they can't really tell what's going on. "Sounds like somebody don't want to go to Spain. You know I can take that away just like that," he says, snapping his fingers. "I'm not going to tell you again. You owe me."

Mr. Speight comes from the classroom and says, "Miss Lashley, inside please." He eyes Greg suspiciously. Greg smiles and pretends to wipe something off my cheek.

"See you later."

My forehead doesn't leave the desk for the entire period. If there were a way to just disappear, I would do it right now. I'd give one of my fingers for Harry Potter's wand. I sneak a glance back at Cherise and catch her staring at me. She looks away and up at the board. Yeah, right, like she's actually listening to what Mr. Speight is saying. Watching her walk by me while I was in trouble is what I'm having the hardest time dealing with. I realize now that I can't depend on anyone or anything.

Well, maybe I'm not all by myself. I still have Garth, and he has got to be the world's greatest tutor. Everything we talked about last night is on the math test. Even better, the first seven questions come straight from those old exams that Garth gave me! These problems used to seem like hieroglyphics to me, and I am breezing through them like nothing. I can still remember the answers, but we have to show all the work. My smile gets bigger and bigger when I finish each question and come up with the right numbers. I glance up at the clock. There are fifteen minutes left in the class and I have three problems left. I can do this.

Question 8 stumps me a little bit. It's different than what Garth and I went over. I try my best, and after erasing a few times, I come up with something that seems to make sense. When I get to question 9, I almost crack a smile. Even though it wasn't one of the questions that Garth gave me, I can hear his voice walking me through it. *When you have a fraction in front of the variable, the easiest way to figure out the value of the variable is to multiply the entire equation by the inverse of the fraction.* That's exactly what I do, and before I know it, I'm writing the answer down. One more question.

I tilt my head back and take a deep breath. I roll my head around a few times, trying to loosen my neck up, and catch sight of someone standing in the hallway near the door. It's Greg. He smiles and winks at me, then walks away. I try to work on that last question, reading the problem over and over. It's pointless.

"Pencils down."

The dark side of school is showing up more and more. News spreads fast at Tech—like a wildfire, to be exact. By fifth period, it seems as if everyone in the school is talking about what happened between Greg and me on Friday. Whenever I walk by a group of people, they start sneezing and saying, "Bless you" before laughing hysterically.

A drawback of going to school with smart kids is that they take ridicule to new heights. One guy turned to his friend and said, "May I pass?" and his friend responded, "Certainly, you have my blessing."

It's bad enough that I am so afraid of running into Greg or Passion. Now I have to deal with the school thinking I'm some kind of whore? I just want to turn and scream at them and tell them what really happened. I want to tell them that Greg is abusive and probably a rapist in the making, if he hasn't done it by now. It's pointless, though, because I know they won't believe me. He is the captain of the basketball team, and I'd be just another girl throwing herself at his feet.

We're inside again for gym today. Looks like soccer is on today. A few of the girls in the class are looking over at me and snickering. They're talking just above a whisper, but I don't pay any attention to them. I'm focused on Cherise.

I tell Mr. S., "I want to play offense." My eyes never leave Cherise. She's the goalie, and I'd love to get one good shot at her head.

"No, we need you at goalie. You're good at catching balls."

All the girls start laughing as the unintentional joke sails right over Mr. S.'s head.

The game isn't much of a distraction. I'm hardly making an effort, because the girls on the other team are as non-athletic as they come. I have no problem swatting away their weak shot attempts.

A girl walks into the gym, and I watch her head straight for Mr. S. It's that girl Azalia from the study abroad office. She hands a note to him and looks over at me as she walks out of the gym. She throws me a nasty glance on her way out of the door. After Mr. S. finishes reading the note, he blows his whistle and pulls me to the side.

"Ms. Lashley, please come with me." When we get out into the hallway, he says, "I just got a note from the principal's office. I'm sorry to tell you this. Something has happened to your brother."

"What? What happened?" I'm so close to crying right now.

"The note didn't say. It just said that you should report to the principal's office immediately." He scratches his head and says, "This is kind of unusual. They don't normally send letters. . . . I'm sorry."

Chapter 26

My heart is racing. Something has happened to my brother. What? Which one? Oh my God, I hope they're not hurt. I hope they didn't get shot or in a car accident. Please just let whoever it is have broken his arm or something. I shouldn't have wished bad things on them. I push through the doors to the stairwell and run full speed toward the stairs. I never make it, because someone grabs my arm.

"Let go of me!"

Greg just smiles at me and pulls me to the other side of the stairwell, the side no one ever uses because it's half a stairwell that doesn't go anywhere.

I'm struggling against his grip, but he is too strong. "Please, Greg, get off me. Something's wrong with—"

"Your brother. Yeah, I know."

"What?"

"I thought I could squeeze you in right before the game, but that ain't happening. I had to think of something to get you out of class."

"What?"

He's laughing now. "Yo, sometimes I amaze myself with my creativity. I thought it might have been a little over the top, but the look on your face is like one of those MasterCard commercials: priceless."

He made it all up so he could get me out of the gym. How could he do something like that? I am so mad that I want to scream, and that's exactly what I'm going to do. "Greg, if you don't get away from me, I am going to scream."

"Excuse me?"

"I *said* if you don't get the hell away from me, I'm going to—"

His hand moves like a blur, and I gag when he grabs my throat. Tears start streaming down my face when he starts taunting me.

"What you was saying now? Huh? I can't hear you. What you was saying?"

I shake my head and mouth the word "nothing" because his grip on my throat is too strong for me to talk.

"Yeah, that's what I thought."

I can feel myself starting to get light-headed.

"Now, when I let go of your neck, are you gonna stay quiet?"

I nod my head.

"You sure?"

I nod my head again and gasp for air when he lets go of my throat.

"Why you have to make things so difficult?" He's smiling and rubbing the side of my face. My body is shaking. "I understand, though. You're just playing hard to get." I try to force a smile, anything that will keep him from hurting me.

"I know we were supposed to wait until after school, but when I saw you this morning, I knew I needed more time with you."

Sweat is dripping from my underarms and running down the side of my body. My heart is beating so fast it feels like it's going to explode.

"Damn, Martine. You got it going on." He has his hands around my waist and he starts to pull me toward him. His face is inches from mine. I'm scared stiff, too afraid to pull back. I feel something vibrating in his pocket. He lets go of me with his right hand and reaches for his phone. After glancing at it, he slides it back into his pocket. "Now I just want you to relax and enjoy yourself." He puts his hand back around my waist and leans in to kiss me. I close my eyes and start praying, asking God to protect me.

Greg is pressed really close to me, but I keep praying. I shudder when he kisses my neck. He pushes me down, forcing me to sit on the stairs, and starts to loosen his belt. His phone goes off again and he says, "Yo, why this broad keep calling me?" He stares at the phone for a few seconds and thankfully decides to answer the call. "Yo, why you blowing up my phone like that, Shorty?"

The volume of the phone is loud enough for me to hear the other person say, "Where are you?"

Greg looks at me, smiling, and says, "I'm just taking care of something real quick."

"I need to talk to you right now."

"Not now. I'll get up with you later."

"Where are you? I wanna talk to you."

He takes a few steps away from me and lowers the volume. He's still between the exit and me. Since I am at the top of the stairwell, I'm trapped. "I just gotta take care of something real quick. I'll talk to you in a little while."

The door swings open and a girl says, "What're you doing back here? Where is she?" She pushes past Greg and comes around the corner, looking up at me. It's Azalia.

She faces Greg and says, "You said that you were going to stop this stuff. You told me I would be the only one." She turns her attention back to me. "Look at her. She's a little kid. What are you doing back here with her?"

"Yo, just chill. It ain't even like that. We was just talking."

She steps in his face and says, "So why is your belt un-buckled?"

He takes a deep breath and looks flustered, because he has no answer. "It's not even like that. We were just talking."

I'm trying my best to find room to squeeze by. Azalia looks like she wants to take a swing at me, but I don't care. I'd rather take my chances with her. I try to push my way by Greg, but he stops me.

"Hold up one second, Martine."

"Please just let me go. I just wanna go."

"Why you stopping her?" Azalia's yelling now. "What were you doing with her back here?"

She starts screaming hysterically and lands a wild punch to Greg's mouth, cutting his bottom lip. Greg grabs her by the face and slams her head against the wall and says, "Yo, what's wrong with you? You bust my damn lip!"

The girls start coming out of the gym and are standing in the stairwell, watching Greg standing over Azalia. She's hunched over crying, holding the back of her head. All the commotion must've caught their attention, because class is not supposed to be over for at least another twenty minutes.

Greg looks up from Azalia and threatens them. "Yo, all of y'all mind your business and go back in the gym."

No one says anything. Everyone's eyes are darting from Greg to Azalia, then to me. With this many students outside of his class, it's only a matter of time before Mr. S. comes out.

"What's going on out here?" Mr. S. says, pushing his way through the crowd of girls.

Greg smiles at Mr. S. and bends to stroke Azalia's face. She pulls away from him and runs through the crowd of girls into the gym. Greg takes off running down the stairs, and Mr. S. goes to the stairwell and yells after him. "You're not going to get away with this, Millons. Not this time." He turns around and says, "Everyone back inside now."

The girls step out of the stairwell and back into the hall-way, but no one goes back into the gym. Nobody wants to miss the show. I wipe my face and push through them. Mr. S. helps

Azalia into his office. He stands by the doorway and says, "Everyone get back to soccer" before shutting the door.

No one bothers moving toward the ball, because everyone is eyeballing me. It's only when I curl up on the mats in the corner that they start talking again, probably about me. I block them out and think about how I'm going to get through the day. How am I going to go through the rest of the school year like this? Besides Garth, I don't have any real friends, and my enemies outnumber him two to one. There's no sense staying in this school and having to be afraid of what's around every corner. On top of that, I have a slut label attached to me that will probably last until my senior year. My dreams of going to Spain are over, so I don't even have that to look to as an escape. I don't want to live like this. When I get home, I am going to tell my parents that I want to transfer out of the school.

Chapter 27

Ms. Barney must have made a copy of my answers, because I hear her using them word for word while she goes over the exam with the rest of the class. I don't even look at the paper, and I jam it into my bag. What's the point? I'm not going to get anywhere close to the number I need for YSSAP after missing that last question on the math test.

"Teenie." I look up after hearing Sohmi call me.

"What?" I skipped lunch. This is the first time I'm seeing her for the day. Cherise burst out for the girls' locker room like a bat out of hell, so I'm sure all the girls know all my damn business by now.

"Can I see your test? Since you're not using it." Sohmi can't really keep eye contact with me. I hand her my bag and zone out again. "Thanks."

Sohmi missed the exam, so God only knows what she's going to do with my test. I don't care. She can do whatever she wants, and if she gets caught, who gives a crap? Thank God Ms. Barney didn't ask me to read one of my essays. My body feels so weak, like I'm about to turn into mush and slide onto the floor. Life is not supposed to be this stressful for someone my age.

When the bell rings, Ms. Barney calls me over to her desk.

"Miss Lashley. May I have a word with you?"

"Yes, ma'am."

"I just wanted to congratulate you on your short essay."

I try to smile and say, "Thank you."

"Let me tell you something, young lady. I hope you consider a career in writing, because you are truly blessed."

Torture, this is just torture.

"So all that's happened since Friday? Geez." Garth has a look of sheer disbelief plastered on his face.

"I gotta get out of this place, Garth. I can't live like this."

"I don't blame you. Maybe that semester away will do you some good."

"I don't think I got the grade I needed in math."

"Oh. I forgot. Was he really standing outside the class?"

I nod my head.

"What a jerk. Hopefully you did well regardless."

"I can forget about YSSAP, Garth. Greg basically told me that if I didn't do what he wanted, he was gonna take my name off the list."

Garth sighs as Mr. Poretsky takes his textbook out of his

briefcase. "Wow, Teenie. I'm sorry that you have to go through this."

I sigh and shake my head.

"Well, let's hope that's the end of it," Garth says.

Yeah, let's hope.

The bell ending ninth period rings.

"Have a great day, class," Mr. Poretsky shouts over the noise of students putting their books away.

As usual, Garth walks me to the center section on the first floor.

"Thanks. I'll see you tomorrow."

"So you're going home now?"

"Yeah. I just wanna take a nap. I might have to go a different way. That crazy girl was waiting for me in the train station this morning."

Garth nods his head, then says, "Well, I don't have anything to do today, so maybe I could take the train home with you."

"Aww, Garth." I touch his arm. "That's so sweet, but you don't have to do that. I'll be fine."

"Somebody has to watch out for you." He smiles, a little hurt by the rejection.

"I appreciate it. You can walk me to the train station if you want."

"Okay. Which way are you going?"

I don't even have time to respond before I'm face-first on the floor. It barely registers that I've been knocked down when I feel someone grab a handful of my hair. I get yanked off the floor and tossed into one of the display cabinets. My knee crashes into one of its metal legs.

"You little ho. You just couldn't stay away from him, could you?"

I turn around and see Passion standing over me. Crystal and her friends are grabbing her and keeping her from hitting me while I'm on the floor. When does this stuff stop?

"I knew you was a little skeezer, but now you went and lied on him and got him arrested?"

"Teenie! Teenie! Leave her alone!" Garth is trying to push toward me, but ends up getting into a tussle of his own with a boy he accidentally knocks down. I lose sight of him in the huge crowd that forms around Passion and me. I look up at her. I know what it's like to deal with ignorant people. No amount of talking is going to settle this. I get up and start backing up but run out of room against one of the walls. Passion gets loose from her friends and walks toward me. I'm trying to find an escape route, but the crowd is much bigger now and I have nowhere to go. She pushes me into the wall.

"Now you gonna get yours. I told you. I told you I hate liars."

The crowd closes in, and instead of keeping my eyes on Passion, I am stupidly looking at them. Where are the security officers? No one here is going to help me, so I close my eyes again and start praying. It worked before—God is going to protect me. Faith the size of a mustard seed, that's all I need.

I see a flash of lightning after she slaps me across the face. My face is stinging, and I go down to one knee. I feel the urge to cry, but I don't. Instead, I think about every other time I've felt bad in my life. I think about all the times that I backed down and didn't say or do anything when people did me wrong. I remember all the times my brothers pushed me around and made me do things I didn't want to do. I think of how Greg assaulted me and I didn't try to fight back. No more.

Passion is leaning over me. She's so close I can smell her breath. "That's what happens when you mess with other people's man. You get dealt with. If I even see you look at him again, you're dead. Do you hear me?" She leans in closer and says it again, "Do you hear me?" I hear the sound of her opening the box cutter and feel her press it against my face. Crystal yells, "No, Passion, don't!"

Passion turns her head to look at her cousin. She's distracted, and I know I have to move quickly. I pull my face back from the blade of the box cutter, and with all the power I can muster, I punch her dead in her face. That one punch is for Cherise turning her back on me, for Greg thinking he could have his way with me, for my brothers and their pranks, for Sabrina and her messed-up comments, for those nasty old men who were looking up my skirt when I was running home, for everyone who ever tried to take advantage of me.

When I hit her, she stumbles and falls back into the crowd, clutching her nose, and drops the box cutter. I pick it up and throw it out of the window into the courtyard. I can see blood running between her fingers before I lose sight of her. Passion's friends have to be around somewhere, so I'm turning my head from side to side, trying to pick them out of the crowd.

The crowd around me lets out a collective "Oh!" after I hit her. I hear a few boys laughing and yelling. Crystal and the other girls are directly in front of me, and I catch sight of Passion again, who is on all fours. Her nose is bleeding really badly. Her friends lift her up from her knees and walk her away from the crowd.

Someone grabs my shoulder, and I turn around ready to swing. Cherise pulls me and says, "Come on, we have to get out of here." The safety officers come running toward the commotion as Cherise ducks my head down and leads me toward one of the stairwells. Garth finally manages to push his way through and follows behind us.

"Where are you guys going? Oh." He bounds up the stairwell when he finally sees that the school safety officers are on their way to the scene of the fight.

"Teenie."

"What?" I can only imagine how mean my face looks.

"I'm really sorry. I . . . I don't really know what I could say to make it up to you but . . . I'm sorry, Teenie."

I'm so angry right now that if Cherise says the wrong thing, I might just punch her in the nose too. "I would never treat you like that. And when you saw Greg grabbing me up in front of class, you didn't even do anything."

"I went and told Mr. Speight that he was bothering you outside the classroom. You're my best friend. I would never let anyone hurt you."

"I'm not your best friend," I snap. "Big Daddy is."

I turn to walk away, but she grabs my shoulder and says, "Wait. I have to talk to you."

"Let go of me." I yank my arm out of her grasp. I don't want her to touch me. I don't want anyone touching me.

"Please, Teenie, just look at me."

I look at her with murder in my eyes. She looks down. "I'm sorry."

"For?"

"For dissing you like that, for not listening to you." Her eyes come up. "You were right, and I didn't want to hear it."

We hear "I think the other girl went this way" coming from below and realize the safety officers are on our trail. We go up a few flights of stairs and come out on the fourth floor. Cherise wanted to go to another stairwell, but I feel safer in the hallway. I hope I don't always have a problem with stairwells.

"You were right about him, Teenie. I'm sorry that I ever doubted you. I don't even know what to say. I am so sorry, and I hope that you'll forgive me for being such an idiot."

In all the years I've known Cherise, I have never heard her apologize.

"So where did this epiphany suddenly come from?"

"I don't know. I guess I was blinded by what I could get out of him."

"Why wait until now to apologize?"

"I was upset that I got in trouble. I wasn't even thinking about what could have happened."

"But why now?"

"Why you smiling like that? It's kinda scary."

"No reason." I take a deep breath and try to mask my inner Glory. Sometimes I forget how much I'm like my mother.

"You know I'm the worst with apologies."

Garth has been way too quiet while I've been talking to Cherise. I look over at him and ask, "Are you okay?" His shirt is ripped and he keeps shaking his head.

"I'm sorry, Teenie. I'm sorry, I couldn't get to you. I—"

"It's alright, Garth."

"Yeah, Garth. Don't worry 'bout her. She clobbered that chick!" Cherise is smiling. "Damn, Teenie, I didn't know you could handle yourself like that. Do you understand what you just did?"

"What?" I look at her and wait for her response, having no clue what she's talking about.

"You just punched the biggest bully in school in her face *AND* made her run away."

"The biggest bully?"

"Yeah. Do you realize how many people that girl has beaten up and robbed?"

Garth definitely remembers his encounter, because I see him rubbing his eye.

"I had no idea."

"She robbed me in the beginning of the year," Cherise says, frowning.

"Really? Why didn't you tell me?"

Cherise looks at Garth and hesitates before I say, "She hit him too."

Cherise nods and continues, "I was embarrassed. I let my

guard down. She was all nice to me, kinda tricked me into trusting her, you know? By the time I figured out what was going on, my earrings and necklace were in her pocket. I felt so stupid for letting it happen."

"Damn."

"Well, whatever. You just blasted her in her face. In front of damn near the whole school!" I can only laugh, because she is throwing wild punches pretending she is fighting.

Then she raises my arm and announces to a couple of approaching students, "The champ is here!" I snatch my hand away and laugh with embarrassment.

"That girl was crazy. I thought she was gonna kill me."

"Did she pull that razor on you? She's notorious for that."

"Yeah."

"Well, why didn't you just give her what she wanted?"

"That's the thing. She wasn't trying to rob me."

"So what the hell did you do to her?"

"Greg."

"Greg?"

"Yeah. . . . Don't you think she had a right to be mad? I was doing stuff with her man. I mean, I didn't know he had a girl but—"

"What? What're you talking about?"

"Greg and Passion. They're boyfriend and girlfriend."

Cherise looks at me like I farted. "Greg and Passion? Come on, Teenie. They call her E-ZPass. That's not his girlfriend. She's a groupie in training, probably trying her best to latch on to a meal ticket."

"So they weren't together?"

Cherise shakes her head and says, "Hell no."

I pick my head up and try to digest the information. "So . . . so she was just some crazy girl that had a crush on him?"

"Yup."

I shake my head.

"I think you should go to the infirmary," Garth says.

"I'm not going to no infirmary. I just want to go home."

"No, Teenie. He's right. You need to go."

"For what?"

Cherise points to my face and it starts hurting again. "Because you have a giant handprint on your face. Plus you have a little cut on your cheek."

I reach to touch a throbbing spot on my face, and when I pull my finger away, I see a little blood. "I didn't even know the infirmary was open after school."

"It is, and you're going."

Cherise and Garth walk with me to the infirmary. Before she lets me go in, Cherise says, "Don't be an idiot and tell the nurse what happened, because if you do, you're gonna get suspended."

"Really?" Suspended?

"Yup. The nurse will tell the dean, and you'll get suspended."

"Oh." I didn't know that. "So what should I say?"

"I don't know. Think of something. Tell her you fell."

I walk into the infirmary and take a seat in one of the raggedy chairs. The nurse doesn't look up from her desk when she says, "Can I help you?"

"Uhh, yeah. I have a cut on my cheek."

Her eyes move from her paperwork and stop at my cheek. The more she stares at it, the more it seems to hurt. "What happened?"

"Umm, I fell."

"You fell?" She stands up slowly and puts on a pair of gloves before rubbing her fingers over the wound. I can tell right away that she doesn't believe me.

"Yes. I fell down the stairs."

"And landed on your face?"

"Yes."

"Did you hurt any other part of your body?"

"No."

"No other part of your body?"

"No." My throbbing knee says otherwise, but I decide to stick to my story.

"Okay, so let me get this straight. You fell down the stairs, not hitting any other part of your body on the way down, and landed on your face?"

"Yes. That's what happened."

"So when were you fighting?"

"I told you I wasn't fighting. I fell." She's staring at me, waiting for me to tell the truth. I'm a terrible liar. "Last period." I end up telling her everything.

"It was *you* who broke that girl's nose?" The way she said "you" makes it pretty obvious that she is having a hard time believing that I did all of that damage. "Well, I'm going to have to file a report. That girl had to go to the hospital, you know."

The nurse frowns at me when I show no sign of remorse.

Chapter 28

I got suspended for the rest of the week. Besides a bloodshot left eye and a tender cheekbone, I'm okay, but I feel horrible about getting suspended. The last time I missed a day of school was when I had the chicken pox in fourth grade, and even then my parents had to fight with me to get me to stay home. Even worse than getting suspended was trying to explain to my mother what I was doing home so early. When I told her I was fighting, she set a scowl on me that made my knees buckle.

"Go up to your room now. Don't even think about turning that TV on. We will talk when your father gets home."

Not being able to watch TV would normally make me mad, but I don't realize how tired I am until I crawl under the covers.

• • •

About an hour later, I hear a tapping sound coming from my window. I walk over to the window and my eyes almost pop out when I see Cherise hunched on my windowsill. She gives me a funny look, telling me to hurry up and open the window.

"Damn, why you take so long to open the window?"

"You scared the crap out of me." I look out the window and try to figure out how she managed to climb up. "Why didn't you just ring the bell?"

"I did. Your mother told me you were sleeping."

"Oh." I look out the window again and ask, "How the heck did you get up here?"

"The tree."

The tree she's talking about has a branch that hangs over our roof. That branch is about five feet above my window. I look up at the branch and look over at her. "You're crazy."

"Yeah, well, we have a lot to talk about."

We certainly do.

"So she ran to the dean's office?"

"Yup. She told them that you broke her nose."

"I bet she didn't say nothing about how *she* started the fight with me."

"Of course not. And I found out why she was coming after you like that." Cherise is shaking her head. I wait for her to continue. "She was all in love with Greg. He had her all gassed up like they were going to get married and whatever, and then he dissed her."

"So what?!?! What does that have to do with me? That's a

reason to be chasing after me like I stole something from her?"

"But you did. Well, kinda sorta. You see, he stopped dealing with her when he started checking for you. I heard he had mad girls. That chick Azalia must've been one of them, but I guess you were one that Passion could finally put a face to."

All I can do is just breathe out. "This is so retarded. Over a stupid boy?"

"There's more. Remember when you were trying to type something to Greg and you sent it to Crystal by mistake? You wrote something about a wild guess, or something like that." I nod my head. "Well, Greg told Passion that he was leaving like ten minutes before that and blocked her, so she thought he was off-line. Passion thought he got off the computer, but then found out he was still online talking to you."

"But how the hell did Passion know that I was— Oh yeah, Crystal ratted me out, didn't she?"

"Yeah, that's kind of foul, but that's her family, so . . . Crystal was telling me a whole bunch of stuff. She says sorry, by the way." I was wondering how Cherise knew all this. "Crystal told me that Passion didn't like you from even before she found out you was messing with Greg."

"Why? I never even said nothing to her. I didn't even know who she was."

"Crystal said she didn't know, and I can't figure that one out either."

"Ughhh! What's wrong with that girl?"

"Passion is so dumb. That's what she gets for giving up the goods like that. That's why they call her E-ZPass." Cherise starts laughing to herself and says, "That name is actually kind of funny." She says it again, "E-ZPass," and continues laughing.

After I hear her say it again, the pieces start to fit. It comes to me all of a sudden. "Cherise, I figured out why she didn't like me. I think my brothers used to deal with her. When they were bringing me home from the park, they saw her by the Laundromat. They probably played her too."

"Wow. That makes sense, though. I heard she got a thing for athletes. Like I said, groupie in training."

"What the hell was she talking about that I got Greg arrested?"

"Oh, you didn't hear about that?"

"Hear about what?"

"Greg got led out of school in handcuffs, crying like a li'l girl."

"What happened?"

"I think Azalia decided to press charges against him. Mr. S. probably talked her into it. I know you heard when he yelled down to Greg, 'You're not getting away with this, Millons.'"

If we weren't talking about something so serious, I would laugh at Cherise's impersonation of Mr. S., because it is on the money. We let that hang in the air and sit quiet for a minute before Cherise says, "So did you hear anything about getting into that nerd program Tree Sap?"

"YSSAP?"

"Yeah."

"Greg basically said if I didn't give him a blessing, I could forget about YSSAP. Like he could get me kicked out of the program or something."

"And how exactly is he gonna do that?"

"He could go and say that he added me to the waiting list and—"

"Teenie, come on. The guy just got arrested. Do you really think anyone's going to believe a word he says?"

"Yeah, I guess you're right. It doesn't matter anyway. I messed up on the math test."

"Really?"

"I needed a ninety-four and . . ." My voice trails off. The highest grade I can get is a ninety, since I didn't answer the last question. That makes me fall short. There's always next year. "I choked. I was on the last question and then I saw Greg standing outside of my class. I just . . ."

"Damn. My man was like a stalker."

"Sounds like we each had one. I've been meaning to ask you . . . Did Big Daddy try to call you again?"

"Hell, no. Your father scared the crap outta him."

"I wish someone would've scared the crap outta Greg, or he would've got arrested before my math test. I can't believe I messed up like that. I just looked up and seen him standing outside the classroom door and I couldn't finish after that."

"Well, don't be so negative. You didn't even see the results yet. Maybe you'll get extra credit or something."

"There was no extra credit."

"Oh. Well, whatever. It probably would've sucked anyway," Cherise says, trying her best to soften the blow. "You should've just tried out for the cheering squad. We'd both end up being team captains."

"I guess that means you made it, huh?"

"Yup," she says, trying not to smile too hard.

"Congrats."

"Thanks. Sohmi and Sabrina made it too. Speaking of Sohmi"—she pauses to take a paper out of her bag and hands it to me—"she said thank you."

"What's she thanking me for?"

"For letting her see the answers to the English test. Did I ever tell you that you're a nerd?"

"Many times."

"Who the hell gets a hundred and ten on a test? Friggin' brainiac."

I got one hundred and ten! I unfold my English exam and see my score. I forgot about the extra credit! "Quick, gimme your phone." Cherise's phone has a calculator on it, and I'm not about to open my bedroom door to look for one. It would be just my luck that my mom would walk by and see Cherise. "If I get a hundred on that American studies paper, then my math score could be like eighty-four and I would still get the scholarship!"

"If? When have you gotten anything but a hundred in Mr. Speight's class? Give me a break."

I grab Cherise around the neck and squeeze her so hard. "I can't believe it! I can't believe it! Okay, okay"—I'm fanning myself—"I mean, I don't know for sure yet but— What's wrong?" Cherise is frowning.

"I don't know. I guess I'll kind of miss you when you go."

"Really? Well, you should've thought about that before when you were acting all stink."

"Yeah, yeah, whatever."

"Hmmph." I grunt with a smirk on my face. I'm mostly joking with her . . . mostly. "Where's my book bag?" The questions that Garth gave me are still in there, so I want to double-check to make sure that I got them right.

"What're you doing?"

Before I have a chance to respond, my mother knocks on the door and pushes into the room. I don't know how Cherise gets under my bed so fast, but she is out of sight by the time my mother gets the door all the way open.

"Martine, who're you talking to?"

"Nobody. I was just rehearsing for a school play." Wow. That one just rolled off my tongue.

"School play? When is it?"

"Oh, they didn't pick the cast yet. I am going to try out for it when I go back."

My mother eyes me with suspicion but lets it go. "Are you hungry?"

"No, Mommy."

Her attention is drawn to the window. "Why you have the window open so wide?"

"I just wanted to get some air in here." Thankfully, from where my mother is standing, she can't see Cherise's bag at the base of my bed. Cherise reaches out and pulls it under just as my mother walks past to shut the window.

My mother closes the window and comes over to me. "Let me see your face." She takes off the Band-Aid and pulls some bacitracin out of her pocket. Iodine and alcohol hurt like hell, so bacitracin is about the only thing I will let her put on my cuts. When she finishes, she walks to the door, but stops and says, "When your father gets home, we're going to discuss this fighting stuff, young lady."

"Aren't you going to be late for work?"

"Never you mind." She pulls the door closed and walks into her bedroom.

"That was close." I didn't even hear Cherise slide from under the bed. "Rehearsing for a play? That was a pretty good one, Teenie." We both cover our mouths to keep from laughing too loudly.

I can't even count how many shocked looks I see on Cherise's face when I tell her about all that's happened to me in the last week. I can see her face going through all the emotions I experienced. She laughs when I tell her what I did with the urn.

"I wish I could've seen the look on Bakari's face."

The laughter doesn't last long once I start telling about everything that happened with Greg. She gets very angry when I tell her about the blessing fiasco.

She frowns a little. "You never heard of a blessing before?"

I look away and shake my head slowly.

"I'm sorry, Martine. I'm so sorry you had to go through that all by yourself." I can tell by her body language that she feels guilty for not being there to help me.

I reach across the bed and grab her hand. Both of our eyes are watering. "You're still my best friend, no matter what."

Cherise leans in and hugs me. "I promise you I will never turn my back on you again."

We don't get to hug for long, because I hear my father come into the house.

"My dad is home."

"How do you know . . . ?" When she hears him singing, she doesn't bother finishing the sentence.

"Just stay here and wait for me to come back up."

"Stay here and do what?"

"I don't know, but you ain't climbing out that window. Just lock the door behind me and put the TV on real low."

"Okay."

"Martine. Come downstairs. Your father is home."

"Okay, Mommy. I'll be right down."

"Where's the remote?" Cherise whispers to me.

"I don't know. Look for it!"

She sucks her teeth before getting serious on me. "You know you can't say nothing to them about what happened with Greg."

I don't respond. I've been trying not to think about it, because it makes me so angry. I know this is not a fairy tale, but it just seems kind of unfair that Greg doesn't get run over by a truck or something. Yeah, he got arrested, but it still doesn't feel like enough.

Cherise repeats herself, saying, "You can tell them about the fight—well, most of it. But no matter what, you can't tell them about Greg."

"Why not?"

"How you think your pops is going to react when he finds out his little princess went into the staircase with Greg?"

"I guess you're right but—" I don't get to finish the sentence because my mother yells again from downstairs.

"Martine!"

"Coming, Mommy."

I tell my parents about Passion and how she slapped me. Whatever questions they ask—like *Have you seen her before?* and *Why was she bothering you?*—I do my best to answer truthfully. It's hard to explain certain things without telling them about Greg, but all I can think about is my dad getting locked up. There's no way I'm telling Beresford about Greg. Besides, he's all into the story when I tell them what happened after school.

"So yah beat she backside?"

"I punched her in the nose, and she started bleeding."

"Serve her right!" He has a huge smile on his face. "Putting her hands on my daughter."

My mother glares at him for encouraging my violence. Beresford tries to chastise me, saying, "Martine, violence is wrong," but he still has a smile on his face, so it kind of defeats the purpose of the statement.

My mother continues to glare at him until he stops smiling. When he's done, she turns to me and says, "Darling, you know you're not supposed to put your hands on people."

"But look at my face, Mommy. She hit me first, and Daddy always told me that if someone hit me that I—"

"Should hit them back." My father's nodding his head as he finishes my sentence. "An eye for an eye."

My mother smiles at my father, the same kind of smile she gave me when I walked in the house with my tight Wade dress. It has a similar effect on Beresford, as he folds his arms and swallows hard. "I don't care who hit who, Martine." She says this to me while staring at my father. After rolling her eyes at him, she turns to me and says, "Violence is never the answer. You should have called one of the safety officers."

"But there were none around, Mommy."

"No hitting. Do you understand me?"

"Yes, Mommy."

"I don't want to hear any more about this. Is that clear?"

"Yes, Mommy."

My parents stand up from the couch, and my mother walks into the kitchen. As soon as she leaves the room, my father pumps his fist and winks at me. I smile at some of the faces that he's making, telling me good job for beating up the bully. He knows that my mother is waiting for him in the kitchen, so he pumps his fist one more time and leaves the room. I can hear him say, "What? I didn't say anything."

My mother is mumbling something to him before my dad comes out of the kitchen holding a chicken leg. While he settles in on the couch, I jump at the chance to talk to my mother alone. I follow her up to her bedroom and say, "Mommy, I have to talk to you."

"Go ahead, sweetie." She's busy fixing herself in the mirror. When she doesn't hear me saying anything, she puts down her comb and sits down next to me. She smiles and says, "What's up?"

I can't do it. I thought I would just be able to walk in here and tell her, but the words won't come out of my mouth.

She looks down at me and says, "Tell me what's on your mind."

"Well. I did something the other day that I am not proud of and it has been bothering me for a little while."

"Okay. What is it?"

"Umm."

She strokes my hair and says, "Take a deep breath and let it out." After I finish the deep breathing, she says, "I will try my best not to get upset."

I nod my head and start talking, but not about the thing that I really want to talk about. "Mommy. I . . . I dumped Beresforda's ashes on Bakari." Her eyes open wide, so I keep talking. "But they were really bothering me. They put shaving cream in my hand while I was sleeping and tickled my nose with a feather so I would smear the shaving cream all over my face. Then Bakari pretended he was sick and—"

She puts her hand up to tell me to stop. "You dumped Beresforda's ashes on Bakari?"

I nod my head and feel ready to cry. "I know I shouldn't have done that. I'm sorry. I know that she was your firstborn and that's the only memory that you—"

"My firstborn?"

"Beresforda was your first child, so I should have had more respect for her remains."

My mother starts laughing like I just told the world's funniest joke. After she calms down, she goes back to the mirror and starts fixing her hair again. "Martine, who told you that Beresforda was my daughter? Never mind. I know one of your silly brothers said that."

"She wasn't my sister? Then who was she?"

"*What* was she is a better question." My mother is still laughing. She stops when she sees the sad look on my face. "I'm sorry, sweetheart. I don't mean to make you feel worse." She rubs my shoulder and says, "Honey, Beresforda was your father's cat."

"A cat?"

My mother starts laughing again. "Do you really think that I would have a child and not talk to you about it?"

"The twins said that you didn't like to talk about what happened to her and that I shouldn't ask you about her."

All she can do is shake her head and smile. "Your brothers are something else. And you really think I would name a child Beresforda?"

"I guess not." I have a scowl on my face and murder on my mind. I don't know how I'm going to get back at them but I am going to spend the next few months coming up with something. They are going to pay for this one.

"Sweetheart, I don't want you to feel bad." She starts rubbing my shoulders but sees that it's having no effect on me. "And, Martine, I don't want you to do anything stupid."

She looks at me until I say, "I won't, Mommy."

"It's probably best if you don't talk to your father about this, dear. He loved that stupid cat."

A freakin' cat?

"Between you and me, most of the stuff in that thing wasn't

252

even the cat's ashes. I didn't have the heart to tell him that those two mischievous brothers of yours broke the urn and then put the dirt from the vacuum cleaner in it. Last time I checked, it was still smelling like Carpet Fresh." My mother starts laughing as she fixes the last button on her shirt.

My brothers are so lucky that they left for school already. Beresford said revenge is a dish best served cold. Those two are in line for some frozen dinners with how bad I'm going to pay them back. I hear my dad lumbering up the stairs.

"Ayy, wha goin on here?" He has his ear to the door of my room. "You got the TV on in there and you out here? I gonna start making you pay the electric bill."

"Martine, I thought I told you no TV?" My mother looks upset.

"I must have sat on the remote when I came out of the room, Mommy. I wasn't watching it."

She's halfway down the stairs when she says, "Okay. Just make sure that doesn't happen again. Unless you want your punishment extended . . ."

"Okay, Mommy. Sorry, Daddy." I walk back to the room and lean against the door. My dad looks at me funny when I kick it twice with my heel. When Cherise unlocks the door, I back in and say to my dad, "It gets stuck sometimes."

Chapter 29

When Cherise decides to leave, she heads over to the window and starts to climb out. It's dark, and the wind is whipping all over the place.

"Umm, Cherise."

"Yeah, I was thinking the same thing," she says before closing the window.

"So how're you gonna get you out of here?"

She thinks for a few seconds and smiles. "I have an idea."

This is one of the few times in my life that I'm happy to be so skinny and lightweight. After we stand at the top of the stairs and listen for Beresford, Cherise puts me on her back and carries me down the stairs. When she first suggested it, I made her explain, because I didn't understand what she wanted to do.

"So there'll only be one set of footsteps."

My dad has the TV blasting, and I tap Cherise, telling her to wait before stepping off the last step. We're about to walk right through my dad's field of view, so I want to be extra careful. I get off of her and peek out and see that Beresford is in the kitchen. Cherise should have no problem getting out. We already hugged at the top of the staircase so we wouldn't risk making any unnecessary noises near the front door. Luckily my father hasn't locked the door for the night. I watched my brothers a while back and learned how to open and close the doors without making any sound. It's kind of tricky, because I have to open the front door and then the security door. This is my first time trying it, and as much as my hand is shaking, I'm able to open both of them without making a sound. Cherise ducks out and heads for the bus stop.

"Martine!"

Oh no. Beresford caught me. I'm going to get in so much trouble.

"Martine!"

"Yes, Daddy?"

He has a puzzled look on his face, and my heart skips a beat when he asks, "Wha you doing by the door?"

"I was about to lock it, but the security door wasn't pulled in all the way." I'm getting better and better at these little lies.

"Oh. I thought you were upstairs. Come and read this." He's holding up his laptop and saying, "Cheese on bread" over and over. "Cheese on bread" is another one of his Beresisms. It can mean that he's happy—like watching the Giants win the Super Bowl—annoyed, angry, or surprised. Judging by the look

255

on his face, I'm guessing he's somewhere between surprised and annoyed.

He's shaking his head, saying, "I can't understand these young men nowadays. They got the whole world in front of them and they do bear foolishness. Why he can't wait until the right time to take money? No kinda broughtupsy."

"Cheese on bread," like "teefin'," is one of the phrases that Beresford uses all the time, but in my book, neither one of them is as creative as "broughtupsy." It's one of my favorites. I can think of a million other ways to say someone has no class. My mother says "no home training," but "broughtupsy" is so much more fun.

Beresford hands me his laptop and points to a breaking news exclusive he's been looking at on the *Daily News* Web site. "It says here that this boy goes to your school. Do you know him?"

"Yes!" I add, "Everyone knows him" when Beresford looks at me funny for the shock I show when I start to read.

BASKETBALL STAR RULED INELIGIBLE
FOR AMATEUR COMPETITION

All-state forward Gregory Millons lost his amateur eligibility this afternoon after it was learned that he was receiving payments from an agent. Millons, a six-foot-four 18-year-old senior who led Brooklyn Tech to the quarterfinals of the PSAL play-offs, has been linked to "street agent" Willis "Stacks" Boykins. Boykins reportedly has ties to several NYC-born NBA players and is under investigation for a myriad of charges ranging from extortion to embezzlement. Receipts obtained by the *News* show several items purchased by Boykins have been found to be in Millons' possession.

So *that's* where he was getting all that money! My brothers did say he was shady.

Millons was set to attend Duke University in the fall on a full athletic scholarship. Calls to Duke University's athletic department have gone unanswered, but a statement from the athletic department is expected tomorrow afternoon, when it is widely anticipated that Millons will have his scholarship offer re-scinded. Sources call the revocation of the scholarship "a foregone conclusion." Messages left at the Millons' residence went unreturned.

"That's dee same boy that hit the game-winner the other day?"

I nod my head, and my dad continues his rant.

"Why he go and do dem things? He couldn't wait?" My father is shaking his head. "Cheese on bread."

My heart is racing so fast that I have to sit down. This is it, the end, where the bad guy gets his. Everything worked out in the end, and on top of that, I might even get the YSSAP scholarship. I should feel better, shouldn't I? Greg got arrested for what he did to Azalia and now he's going to lose the one thing he loves most. Thinking about that should make me feel great, but I can feel myself forcing a smile. I should be jumping for joy right now. So why don't I feel any better? Why do I want to cry? Why did I want to cry as soon as I read his name in the paper?

The phone rings a few times, but it's muffled. It takes my father a few seconds to realize he's sitting on it.

"Lashley residence. Hold a moment. It's Cherise."

He goes to hand me the phone. There's no way I'm putting that thing next to my face. "I'll take it upstairs, Daddy." I run up to my room and yell down, "Got it." I wait to hear the click of the phone downstairs before I start talking. Since the Big Daddy fiasco, Beresford has been monitoring my communications like the CIA. "Hello."

"Hey."

"Where are you?"

"I'm on the bus. I'll be home in a few minutes. Yo, your mom almost saw me."

"My mother? How? She should be at the hospital by now."

"Well, I don't know where she *should* be, but she pulled up at the light and I had to hide behind a car so she wouldn't see me. She turned onto your block just now. She should be walking in any minute."

Sure enough, I hear my mother keying into the house a few seconds later. She's grumbling to herself as she runs into her bedroom. I hold the phone away from my ear while I listen

258

to her rummage through the junk on top of her dresser. Cherise has been busy talking about how some guys were trying to talk to her at the bus stop. I cut her off and say, "I'm going to tell."

"What?"

"I said I'm going to tell my mother what he did to me."

"No, Teenie. I'm telling you. Don't say nothing. Trust me. I would never steer you wrong."

"Not this time, Cherise. I have to."

"But why?"

"Because I have to. I don't want to feel bad anymore."

"You'll get over it. I'm telling you. You might get in trouble if you say something."

"Maybe. But if I don't tell, I know I'll be in *real* trouble."

"How?" I don't bother to answer, because I know she won't understand. After a few seconds she says, "Okay, your funeral."

"No, it is *not* my funeral. This is something I need to do for me and it's what I'm going to do, so don't go trying to convince me to do something else."

"Okay, okay. My bad. Take it easy. I'm sorry."

"It's okay."

She pauses for a few seconds and says, "Okay. Love you, Teenie. My battery is about to d—" before her phone cuts off.

My mother zips by my room and down the stairs toward the front door. God only knows why she came back home, but the fact is she's here. If I wait another day, I know I'll find some way to talk myself out of telling.

I'm standing at the top of the staircase when I call her. "Mommy."

"Yes, Martine?" Her back is to me and she is stuffing her foot into her shoe while she reaches for the front door.

"I need to talk to you."

"Can it wait? I'm really late for work."

"No. I need to talk to you right now."

"You're just like your father, you know. Stubborn as a mule." She turns around and glances at her watch. She puts her bag down, sighing. "Alright. I'm already late as it is."

Tears stream down my face as I say, "I think we'd better sit down."

acknowledgments

God, my wife (my rock), Mommy *(thank you for all of your sacrifice)*, Alphonzo *(thank you for being a trailblazer)*, Isis, Gibran, and Tiye Grant, Raymond and Maureen Gittens (thank you for allowing me to share your home while I found myself), Enrique, Kwayera, Uwingablye, Solwazi, and Bakari Cunningham, Daniel and Natasha Flores (I will never forget what you guys did for me), Chad Gittens, Lawrence and Violet Archer, Marcy Posner, Erin Clarke, Machel Smith, Tricia Smith, Aisha Havill, the Smith family, the Simmons/Brooks family, Stacey Barney, Larry and Judy Gutman, Ronnie Stolzenberg, Cecile Goyette, Joseph and Azalia Speight, Enrique and Safiya Simmons, Jackie Carter, Jumaane Ford, Allison Grant, Jovone Simmonds, Andrez Carberry, Kim Francis, Shawnda Bailey, Raelene Lazarus, Andre Mais, Tameka Lyons, Adrian and Nancy Florence, Richard "Skane" Ford, Kevin L. Phillips, Maisha Dang, Crystal White, John and Sahar Harris, Oshadi Kelly, Pat Spencer, Golan Shlomi, T3 Capital, Brian Carey, Ignacio and Ivy Tzoumas, Bruce Baskind (Best American Stud Teacher ever), Garson Grant, Lartif Thornton, Cesar Rivera,

Anthony "PJ" Davis, Latia Holder, Aisha Saunders, Frank and Linda Gittens, Desiree Medas, the Grosvenor/Sisnett/Phillips/Buckmire family, Derek Gardner, Rumi Kitagawa, Jeff Cox, Ira Brustein, Heather Karaman, Gloria Zicht, Edgardo Lugo, Khalilah Gibbs-Harrington, Janelle Daniel, Joyal Mcneil, Lyshaan Hall, Maurice Malone, Nytaino Romulus, Jean-Marc and Edwidge Dejoie, Randy Gittens, Yolanda Sangweni, Colin Channer, Sabine Jovin-Tourenne, Jason and Danyale Robinson, Euken Gabriel, Jerreno Pope, Ogo Nwanyanwu, the Taitt family, Vinita Neves, Oscar Alcantara, Othniel Taitt, Roy Roberts, Sean Hannon, Shellane Semple, Edmire Saint-Pierre, Sam Kornhauser, Ryan Rabaglia, Curtis Charles, Lou Forte, Larry Sackler, Michael Streiker, Alex Mizan, Antonio and Anita Gholar, the George family, Chris Holko, Rashida Dorant, the St. Lawrence family, Edward Meertins-George, Toby Thompkins, Simone Thornhill, Solan James, Tamyka Clarke-Cox, Nicole Yarde, Matthew Kenny, Ayanna-Abena Cox, Vicki Haddow, Courtney Pierre, Martin Dixon, and all the people that let me borrow pens on the subway.